ORIGINAL SINNER

SHARITA RUSSELL

NATTERJACK PRESS

Copyright © 2021 by sharita russell

All rights reserved.

No part of this book may be reproduced in any form or by any electronic or mechanical means, including information storage and retrieval systems, without written permission from the author, except for the use of brief quotations in a book review.

ISBN: 978-0-6451851-0-2 (paperback edition)

ISBN: 978-0-6451851-1-9 (ebook edition)

For Jenni, Nat and Luke.

CONTENTS

1. Limbo — 1
2. Greed — 9
3. Gluttony — 19
4. Blasphemy — 31
5. Heresy — 39
6. Idolatry — 46
7. Perjury — 50
8. Fraud — 57
9. Sacrilege — 65
10. Simony — 78
11. Violence — 84
12. Wrath — 92
13. Pestilence — 99
14. Malignity — 112
15. Envy — 119
16. Apocrypha — 127
17. Pride — 135
18. Lust — 147
19. Covetousness — 152
20. Treachery — 166
21. Despair — 170
22. Apathy — 174
23. Heartsease — 181

Acknowledgments — 189
About the Author — 191

1

LIMBO

> The average man does not know what to do with this life,
> yet wants another one which will last forever.
> Anatole France, *The Revolt of Angels*

NO ONE COMES THIS WAY BY ACCIDENT. There is nothing special to draw the eye. The curve of the highway encourages a driver to hug the bend and keep driving through the desert that stretches horizon to horizon. Yet, concealed behind tufts of scrubby grass, a faint line of gravel snakes from this curve into god-forsaken country.

Every year, I take that gravel track. At Samhain. It is my duty to show up and perform. But today I pause. I suffer a moment's doubt as my hand hovers above the indicator. Almost too late, I swerve onto the unbeaten path.

Tires spit gravel. My truck bounces along this angry welt, drawing me away from civilization. Nothing to see but the occasional grass tuft or bleached rock shimmering in the heat. I am sweating inside my old truck. I wind down the window. Dust pours in. It cakes in the corners of my eyes and tightens the skin on my cheeks.

A couple of miles further and the ground sharply inclines. The engine strains. There's a trick to getting into second gear—I slam my foot on the clutch and jiggle the stick until it finds the right niche. I press down on the accelerator and the engine roars. The truck jolts forward. In the rearview mirror, a plume of red dust rises behind me.

I know he sees it too.

This would be the moment to turn back. A crackle of static bursts from the radio followed by the strident chords of Saint-Saëns' "Danse Macabre." I turn off the radio—I don't need another reminder of my foolishness.

At the crest of the hill, I pause. I see to the horizon and there is nothing in this wasteland but my destination: a junkyard sitting stark against the emptiness. It is a graveyard of rusting metal—of abandoned washing machines, cathode-ray tube televisions and fridges, restrained by a sagging wire fence. Although there is no breeze, the wire waves back and forth between loose posts, beckoning.

I coast towards the stacks of tires framing the entrance. Behind them, old clothes dryers sit on dishwashers—an upper and lower set of chipped teeth. I head towards a brick wall daubed with crudely drawn graffiti: villains and superheroes battle in cloaks, 'kapow' and 'bam' blazoned above their heads. My mouth dries and my stomach knots. The architect of this junkyard enjoys a joke at my expense.

The track narrows and swings inward, a Fibonacci spiral taking me to the heart of this place. Sunken, blackened, and pitted, the ground bears the scars of my previous visits—a huge, burned circle. Evidence of thousands of bonfires. The stench of burning tires and diesel is ingrained in the dirt.

I hit the brakes and my truck comes to a halt a short

distance from the burned circle. One final shudder and the engine clunks silent. I lean my shoulder into the door and yank the handle. I scoop up my pack of Gauloises cigarettes from the passenger's seat and jump out.

I light a cigarette and inhale, relishing the poisons that course through me. My heart speeds and my brain slows. Nicotine calms me. I draw comfort from the dark tarry blend, unfiltered and robust, that I've smoked for decades. I purse my lips and send a smoke ring drifting towards the setting sun. Time is running out. One last drag before I grind my cigarette into the dirt.

Dressed in white, he is perched on a stack of tires, one leg planted, the other dangling. His eyes are narrowed against the sinking sun that casts a long, twisted shadow behind him. Its hue accentuates his blond locks. His shirt clings to muscular arms crossed at chest height, one shoulder higher than the other. White and gold, incongruous against the backdrop of rust and rubber, his calm stirs deep panic in me. He shouldn't be here yet.

I've known him for as long as I've been alive. I know to fear him when something is different. I nod, but my palms are damp as I reach for another cigarette.

He stands and saunters over, hand outstretched.

'Can't you buy your own?' I toss him the pack and he taps one onto his palm. He grins his perfect smile, full lips, white teeth, purses those lips and blows. Both our cigarettes light. My hand trembles as I bring mine to my mouth and inhale.

'You're early,' I mutter.

'You're late.'

The hair on my neck prickles. My heart pounds so loud I'm sure he can hear it.

'Something's different about you.' His tone is matter of fact.

I cough as my throat constricts on the smoke.

'It's been a tough year,' I say. 'How was yours?'

He laughs. 'Small talk, Eve?'

My cheeks grow hot.

There are flecks of gold in his dark irises. Eyes rimmed by long lashes, eyes that see too much. I glance away, unable to sustain his gaze. I want to tell him my decision. Get his reassurance that I'm doing the right thing. But I already know his opinion—he tells me every year. Give up. Walk away.

'I see you're using blue beech this time. Harder to get going than the oak and pine.' He tilts his head at the logs piled in the back of my truck. I stand between him and the logs: I don't want him to look too closely.

'Yes, I'm hoping it burns longer and hotter. Better combustibility, according to the internet.' There is another reason—it's better to carve, softer than oak, harder than pine, but I don't want him to guess my plan.

'Don't leave it too long to get started. Those demons are raring to go.'

'I know what I'm doing.'

'I'm sure you do.'

He laughs and plants a kiss on my cheek. His smoky breath smells of apples. Electricity snaps against my skin. He inhales until the tip of his cigarette glows incandescent orange. The paper flares and shrinks, the glowing strands of tobacco twitch as they perish and the stick burns to half its length. He doesn't exhale.

I wonder if nicotine affects him or if it is just for show. He grins and my heart beats faster. He's worse than any drug. Standing too close, radiating, he invades my space. I step back. No one is immune to Lucifer's charm.

'You're in the way.'

Hands up, he walks backward.

I take a final drag on my cigarette, crush the butt under my heel and walk around to the back of the Dodge. Although I try to appear confident, I falter as I reach for the wood. I wish he would leave. I hope he won't. His scrutiny borders on predatory, but I ignore him, focus on my task. He doesn't offer to help and anyway, I'm not sure if that's against the rules.

I've perfected pyre building over the years. It's a jigsaw and each piece has its correct place. I marked every log and loaded them in reverse sequence into my truck. There's a rhythm to the unloading; lift, check, place, lift, check, place. An old-fashioned waltz plays in my mind. I plug the gaps with tinder and paper and douse the pyre with diesel.

When I am done, I take a step back to examine the bonfire that towers over me. I am hot, sweaty, my hair stuck to my forehead. Lucifer circles the structure, appraising my handiwork.

'I think this might be your best one yet, Evie.'

I like it when he calls me that. His delicious aroma of ozone and sun-kissed skin and sex overtakes my senses. I adjust a perfectly placed log and take a deep breath.

'Good to hear, as this will be my last.'

The expression of surprise on his face gives me satisfaction. He didn't expect me to quit, although he's been goading me to do it since the beginning. For his gain, not mine. I'm the rope in their tug of war. Him and God. His eyes widen as he waits for details. I give him none.

'Why bother at all with tonight's fight? You've finally come to your senses. Let's go celebrate.'

I shake my head. 'One last hoorah. Working my notice.'
'Dutiful Eve,' he says.
'Just tying up loose ends.'
'Yes, those loose ends. You know what this means, what if—?'

He need not finish. I've asked myself the same question many times. What if God doesn't grant the one thing I've fought for all these years? After tonight, I won't be back and my dream will be gone.

The last finger of sunlight clings to the horizon. One final flare brings the junkyard to life and every aspect of his construct is illuminated. Shadows hover, waiting to reclaim their territory. A mist is rising as the heat from the desert sand curdles in the cooling air. From the corner of my eye, I see the graffiti on the wall shift and the superhero's cape waft.

'I have to prepare,' I say. The shadows shift at my words pressing closer with eagerness.

Lucifer glows in the gloom, burning from within. 'I'm not stopping you.'

'You wanna watch me pray?'

He shudders. A wink and he's gone.

Even without his presence, it is harder than usual to focus. I rummage in the cab of the Dodge, moving things needlessly until I can think straight again. That little voice in my head tells me it is not too late. Run away.

I look beyond the junkyard at the darkening desert and contemplate the long drive to the highway. The urge is so strong, I wonder if it's Lucifer's influence. But I can't walk away from my last chance at absolution.

In the centuries before my vigil, demons swarmed through those gates beside the dead, eager to wreak havoc until dawn. Men of God would daub the blood of sacrificial lambs on their doors and pray through the night. The unwary went to their beds and suffered night-terrors as demons fed them twisted dreams, causing delusions and mania. But another type of human welcomed these nocturnal visitations. They allowed the corruption to seep into their minds and souls and out through their actions. The world is a safer place since I began my vigil.

In the passenger seat footwell is a box with my armor and my Ulfberht sword. There's not much armor; just my leather brigandine and greaves. Demons fight with tooth and claw, not steel, and although both are razor-sharp, their speed and strength are their greatest weapons, and I can't be weighed down. Demon skin needs no protection. The runes on my sword are the only reason it slices through their hide. My scythe through their rye.

I am a creature of habit and my pre-battle rituals have grown over the years, giving me comfort albeit while my rational mind mocks me. A tiger's eye sits in my pocket for luck, the smooth stone cool and heavy. My sword must lie on the ground, pointing towards the graffiti wall. I kneel before the pyre to light a candle and burn incense. The resin catches, a blend of sandalwood, frankincense and myrrh. It glows amber as I blow on it, releasing snakes of smoke that intertwine for a moment before dissipating. Its perfume masks the current bouquet of burned rubber and diesel.

I stand and walk clockwise around the unlit pyre. Three times. Each time offering my service to God. Asking Him to bless and protect me in the battle ahead, hopeful for a sign that my help is no longer needed, my penance fulfilled. He doesn't reply. Time to turn and walk anticlockwise. Three times. Reconfirm my commitment to the task ahead. I ask forgiveness for the taking of life, regardless of its form. My plea for absolution and an end to this penance draws no response.

Those familiar pangs of bitterness rise at the resounding silence. It no longer matters. Tonight is my last fight.

2

GREED

People who comprehend a thing to its very depths rarely stay faithful to it forever. For they have brought its depths into the light of day: and in the depths there is always much that is unpleasant to see.
Friedrich Nietzsche, *Human, all too Human*

My bonfire needs to be lit before dark and must be blazing before the gates open. I twist newspaper from my pocket as a taper and touch it to the candle flame. One hand cupped against any stray breeze, I bring fire to my pyre. The paper burns too fast. An orange ribbon of flame consumes it. Holding its blackened form for a moment, it disintegrates. I fix another taper, longer and thicker than the last, and thrust it deep into the kindling. The wood shavings smoke but refuse to light. A third time, but neither twig nor tinder responds to my ministrations.

I am no novice. I know how to light a fire. Ghostly shadows hover. Watching. Waiting. Laughing. Fire is my only ally in the upcoming battle. They'd like to see me fight without its light and protection.

'Lucifer!' I call out.

He appears without delay. 'You rang, mi' lady?' His eyes flick to my unlit pile of sticks.

'Did you tamper with my bonfire?'

A tilt of his head. 'I told you, beech takes longer to catch.'

'It won't catch at all.'

'Maybe it's a sign.' His chin jerks upward. He trails a finger across one log and small sparks fly. The same finger traces down my arm and every nerve in my body tingles. I jerk from his reach.

He smiles and strolls off. I breathe again. With shaking fingers, I pull my hair out of its elastic band, smooth back the stray hairs and re-tie it high on my head. My palms flatten imagined creases from my worn jeans.

'Nice jeans,' he says as he circles back. In the encroaching gloom, his eyes shine as he watches my every move. He's wearing denim too now, dark and expensive, and it shows off his legs to perfection. Swift steps bring him back to me. He's planning something, I can see it.

'Everything looks fine to me.' His eyes linger everywhere. His lips smile.

I step back. Every minute he delays my preparations is an advantage for his demons. The fog that collects around our feet hisses and surges forward, smothering my pyre with roiling tentacles.

That small voice in the back of my head whispers—*It's not worth it. Get in your truck and drive away.*

I look over to the Dodge. The patchy paintwork, dents and rust. My stalwart companion since she rolled out of the Dodge Brothers' showroom on Hollywood Boulevard in 1936. It's time for us both to retire.

He looks too. 'You should get rid of that pile of junk.'

'She's like me. Keeps on going.'

He scoffs. 'Breaks down all the time. Belongs in a museum.'

'Nothing a little TLC can't fix.'

His eyes darken.

'Will a little TLC fix you?'

I look down at my hands, rough and calloused, my nails jagged and dirty. My shirt is threadbare, jeans torn, and my boots are sturdy and practical. His words hit a nerve.

'I'm fine as I am,' I say, swallowing the lump in my throat.

He steps closer, shocking me with static as his arm brushes mine. I force myself not to flinch.

'Don't you miss the admiring glances? Compliments? The dresses, hats, and shoes? You must miss the shoes!'

'I prefer to be comfortable.' I stare past him, determined to focus on some imaginary spot out beyond the perimeter of the junkyard.

'Looks more like complacence. Remember what it feels like to be romanced?'

'By whom—you?' I realize my mistake as the words leave my lips.

HE TAKES my hand and before I can speak, the junkyard and the half-light of dusk are gone. In their place are bridges and piers, bathed in sunlight. The gentle slap of water against stone is accompanied by a briny breeze and the excited hum of voices. We stand by the Grand Canal, Venice. Behind us, lies St. Mark's Square. Tourists in sunhats with cameras scurry across the marble piazza, forming a haphazard assortment of queues and clusters. None of them notice us.

My jeans and shirt are now an evening gown, cinched at my waist with my shoulders bared to the warm evening. I toss my head in disbelief, and a perfumed riot of curls falls forward. Disorientated by the sudden shift in location and the motion of the water, I clutch at Lucifer's arm. I see my hands—red fingernails, diamond rings. I realize my balance is altered by the stiletto heels I wear instead of my boots. Earrings weigh heavy in my lobes and a heady musk surrounds me; night jasmine and rose, a combination from centuries ago. It's touching he remembers.

Lucifer cups my elbow. He's dressed for dinner—white shirt, dark tailored suit, and Hermes tie with little flames. I am surprised how beautiful he looks.

'This is how you should look.' His voice is husky as he slides his hand from my elbow to my wrist. He brings my hand to his lips—a featherlight brush against my knuckles. There is a meridian that runs from the fingers to the heart, and mine is ablaze. I try to extract myself from his grip, but his fingers hold tight. 'Life doesn't have to be a struggle, Eve. It isn't a sin to take care of yourself, or to let someone else do it.'

A gondola awaits us. The gondolier extends his arm to help me board. I open my mouth to refuse but Lucifer preempts.

'Indulge me.'

'I don't want to play your game.' That flutter of my pulse belies my words. The overt seduction scene, obvious manipulations, anger yet flatter me. It would be easy to succumb to his attention. I want to know what his game is, to understand his true purpose in bringing me here.

Although, the thought of snuggling up to him in a gondola is more appealing than fighting demons.

He frowns. 'Are you afraid you might enjoy yourself?' His throaty whisper hints at more. 'When did you last do something for no reason other than pleasure?'

Nothing recent comes to mind. 'Take me back.'

'Why, Eve?' A gentle question.

Tears prick my eyes. I am more afraid of being here with him than facing a horde of demons. There's no sword or armor to bolster my defenses. That twisting, gnawing panic grips my stomach. I've been down this road before with Lucifer and it never ends well.

'Are you planning on keeping me here all night so I can't fight?'

'Only if you wish it.'

'I don't wish it. What if tonight is the night He says yes?'

'You don't believe that any more than I do,' Lucifer whispers behind me. His scent invades my senses, and his breath warms my ear. My focus is on his hands, the one at my waist, and the other on my shoulder, burning against my skin. I lean forward, agitated by the press of his body against my back.

Pigeons rise as one from the piazza, silhouetted against the pinking sky. St. Mark's Cathedral is on the right of the square, bathed in holy light, the setting sun's benediction.

'He's not worth it. He doesn't deserve your loyalty.'

'Stop it.'

'I would not treat you so, not abandon you to loneliness nor ignore you, sweet Evie. You deserve love. To be truly loved.' His lips burn a trail of kisses against my neck. Each kiss awakens a memory of pain, a torment from which I long to be rescued. I shudder and push his lips away. The skies darken.

Millions of tiny pearls rain from the sky, pattering against the marble slabs in the square. They plop into the churning waters of the canal.

A tour group passes nearby, and the guide opens her umbrella. 'Was that rain? I thought I felt a drop,' she says. She scurries on, her charges in tow, a worm wending its way through the crowd. I feel Lucifer's smile against my ear.

'Do you need proof of my devotion? A little bling around your neck, at your wrists and ears?' His hot breath brushes my earlobe, quickening the pulse at my throat. It is a struggle to calm my ragged breathing and pounding heart. I lean back against him and hear a guttural sound of satisfaction from his throat.

'How can He send you out to face death, year after year? I don't like to see you battered and broken. Let me take care of you.' His voice is liquid tenderness. Promises wrapping me, soothing me, and lulling me into wanting more. I am not weak-willed, or unable to resist the forktongued charms of a philanderer. These are words I have longed to hear from another. From the one whose forgiveness never comes.

'Say the word, Evie, and your life will change for the better. A life of indulgence and abundance is yours for the asking. Let me spoil you. Let me treat you as you should be treated.'

'Please stop.' I believe every word he utters. It is the sincerity in his voice that beguiles me. He is good at sincerity. 'Take me back.'

He releases me and steps back. The cold rushes in between us.

'What happens after tonight, Eve?'

I have asked myself that question many times. What becomes of my life if there is no battle on Samhain? It has been my all-consuming quest for centuries. No more demons. No more Lucifer. No more hope of absolution. Without my penance, what am I?

'I don't know.' I hate the way my voice breaks over those three little words.

'He's abandoned you.' Lucifer speaks without the malice I've grown to expect.

I bite back a sob.

'He doesn't love you, Eve. Not like I do.'

There are gasps behind us as a gaggle of girls rush past, phones flashing in our direction. Lucifer flashes me a smile and steps back.

'It's her! I'm sure it is.'

A girl steps from the pack. 'Can I take a selfie?'

She doesn't wait for a reply but presses her head close to mine and snaps a photo. She checks the shot and I see my clothes have changed to designer daywear; a Chanel jacket over a Fendi dress. My hair is styled, my makeup immaculate. I look elegant, unlike me.

'I'm such a fan,' she gushes. Her friends scream as they pull her back into their fold, grabbing at her phone.

'This way, *signora*.'

The gondolier is wearing a captain's hat, and the vessel is now a sleek motorboat. I don't want to step aboard but there is a commotion in the square as more people think they recognize me. Phones raise and point in my direction, hundreds of clicks, some flashes. The crowd presses in.

Lucifer smiles and steps onto the boat, holding out his hand. I peer at the interior of white leather and polished walnut. Champagne and caviar wait on ice. The engine is purring.

'Your jet is waiting,' he says. 'Dinner in Paris?'

'Not interested. I've done the rich thing before.' The pontoon shifts with the engine's wave.

'In Sumeria. It's different today. Much better toys.'

The crowd inches closer. I can feel them behind me, a mounting frenzy in the air as they clamor for a glimpse, a touch. Someone throws flowers in my direction.

'Get ready for the mob.' He's still smiling as he pulls me across the gap onto the deck. The idling motor kicks into life. The crowd goes crazy.

'Wave to your fans.'

'I'm not interested in celebrity either.'

'Riches, fame, they are mere stepping stones to what we really want. Adoration, Eve. Bask in the love He denies you. I would make all on Earth and below bow before you.'

'Don't be ridiculous.' A tendril works its way past my resistance. How nice it is to be appreciated, to be noticed. For too long, I've lived from one Samhain to the next. Alone.

I stare back at the figures crowded on the pontoon, waving. I remind myself they are compelled by Lucifer. His illusions are not enough for me. The widening expanse of water brings comfort and the tightening in my chest loosens.

My fingers rub over the polished railings on the deck and the wood brings to mind the shabby interior of my Dodge. The contrast of this Eve and my often shabby exterior. From tomorrow, I must choose a different life. Why not the one he offers?

'I know you better than you know yourself, Eve,' he whispers. His fingers burn against my skin and my body betrays me and responds. There is nothing shabby about our chemistry.

'Give me tonight to prove it to you,' he urges. 'Stay here

with me.' Lucifer pulls me tighter, crushing me against his chest.

He is aware of his magnetism; he uses it to toy with me. Conflict rages within every cell. Physical proximity to an angel is like being set on fire and caught in ice at the same time. Desire and terror seep from every pore. It would be so easy to say yes. To walk away from the battle I hate and enjoy a night of pleasure. His fingers caress my skin, stirring primeval desires. The thought of being Lucifer's queen terrifies me. Thrills me. He's tempted me before, but not so ardently of late. This reminds me of another temptation and the consequences haunt me still. No, this is different. I'd like to believe, maybe, he does love me. I kiss him back.

'You belong to me.' His triumphant words hit me like cold water. A reminder of the gulf between us: not just angel and human, but male and female. That cockiness he gets when he thinks he's right pulls me back from the precipice. I walked away from ownership long ago.

'Take me back,' I say a third time.

A deep growl escapes his twisted mouth. He clenches his fists and there is steel in his stare. Dark clouds roll in and thunder claps overhead. Water churns beneath us. 'Always duty over love, Eve. Duty to God, duty to Adam. No wonder you're miserable. I offer an end to suffering but you wear your misery like a lifejacket.'

I close my eyes to stop the tears. 'Can't you see? All I ever wanted was to go back.'

His laugh is bitter. 'And you're no closer to that happening than the day you were banished. The cockamamie plan you've been working on for the last two thousand years has got you nowhere. As if the father wasn't bad enough, you went and listened to the son! You'll fight tonight and then what? Are you ready to walk away from thousands of years of commitment with nothing to show for it?'

'Tonight is my last battle.' I am adamant. 'Eden was the only thing I wanted, but I can't do this anymore.'

'The only thing?'

I nod.

His expression changes. His eyes lighten to pure gold and a slow smile curves his lips. The water of the canal lies smooth as glass.

'If I give you Eden, will you choose me?'

3

GLUTTONY

Of Mans First Disobedience, and the Fruit
Of that Forbidden Tree whose mortal tast
Brought Death into the World, and all our woe,
With loss of Eden, till one greater Man
Restore us, and regain the blissful Seat...
John Milton, *Paradise Lost*

PEOPLE THINK HE APPEARED TO ME AS A SNAKE, BUT that isn't true. Lucifer appeared in human form, a living David with angelic countenance. And I, slack-jawed and numb-tongued, welcomed him into my heart. Dazzled first by his beauty and then his manner, I succumbed to his honeyed words and gestures. It never occurred to me that his intentions might be corrupt. All was fair in Eden, even the snakes, and my naivety devoured and returned his adoration without question.

I took him to my favorite spot by the river where I spent my afternoons. He held my hand as we watched the sunlight play with the lazy current and leave a trail of sparkling kisses over the rippling water. Our fingers were awkward in their initial twining: his warm and confident, mine clammy. But Lucifer soon put me at ease. He shared my infectious joy in the world's wonder: a rabbit's twitching ears and nose in the undergrowth, berries plump in their tight skins bouncy on the bramble, a magpie's beady eye peering at us through glossy leaves.

We sat by the riverbank and the long grass prickled against my thighs. I watched his fingers as he picked daisies and fashioned chains for my neck and wrists, a circlet for my hair, rings to hang about my ears. It was nice to have a companion willing to do the things I liked. Adam preferred hiking to high ground, climbing rocks and chasing deer. The times we spent as a couple involved me accompanying him on his pursuits. Or fucking. For Adam, that too was an energetic pursuit. That afternoon, I wasn't a sexual plaything or a subservient companion, neither an afterthought nor a thoracic construct. I was Eve, Goddess of the Afternoon.

After Lucifer crowned me queen for the day, we swam in the cool stream and let the sunshine toast us. Laziness descended, broken only by the plop of an occasional fish breaching the mirrored surface of the stream to snap at dragonflies darting beyond reach.

He lay on his back, eyes closed, and I seized the opportunity to examine the soft rise and fall of his chest, the flat smoothness of his belly, the jut of his chin. With eyes still shut, his fingers sought mine. They gripped tight, pulling me down beside him as a smile played on his lips. I laughed and snuggled under his arm, and closed my eyes.

When I awoke, the sun hung lower in the sky and Lucifer was sitting up, watching a kingfisher hover over the water.

'Would you like to see my favorite place?' he asked.

'Please,' I said. I didn't want my time with him to end.

He took my hand, and we ran breathless towards the densest part of the Garden.

I stopped at the edge of the ring of trees. Adam had forbidden me from entering this place in a voice stern and dreadful. His terror infectious, I obeyed.

Lucifer showed no fear. His hand was warm in mine, and he drew me in, made me bold. He was eager to share and that excited me.

The trees grew close together here. Their branches wove a thicket to hinder sunlight. Vines climbed the length of their trunks, long, sickly fingers clinging to the bark. My nostrils filled with the damp of rotting leaves and musty loam. It was cool under this dense canopy, and my skin prickled with goosebumps. My toes grew cold in the damp soil.

The unfamiliar chirp of insects was so pervasive, my pulse joined their symphony. A random hoot from a lone creature cut through the cacophony, silencing it for a semibreve rest before the symphony recommenced. Only the pressure of his hand in mine kept me from running.

We stopped at a clearing at the center of this dense hub, where a giant tree towered, the ruler of its domain. In the graceful spread of its branches, sunlight twinkled against the glossy leaves that grew in abundance, concealing the many birds that made their homes on its boughs. Fragrant blossoms, gossamer among the green, nestled beside clusters of shiny spheres, a riot of white, green and red. Glad to be out of the gloomy forest, my spirits lifted at the sight until the significance of the tree dawned on me.

I had the urge to turn and flee but Lucifer gripped my hand, his thumb tracing slow circles against my palm. Pulling me with him, he sauntered up to the gnarled bark of the trunk. My pulse raced faster than it had with the insects. With all the force of my body I resisted him.

'It can't hurt you,' he whispered. 'What have you heard of this place?'

'Is this the Tree of Knowledge, or the Tree of Life? Adam says both are forbidden to us,' I said.

He raised an eyebrow and one side of his mouth twitched. 'Knowledge and Life are two aspects of the same tree. One begets the other. Why should either be forbidden to you?'

'He didn't say.'

'What else did Adam tell you?'

'I'm not to touch it nor eat its fruit, or I shall suffer.'

'Adam lied, Eve,' he said.

Before I could stop him, he pressed my palm against the bark, his hand covering mine keeping it in place. With a gasp, I snatched my hand back, scraping against the wood in my haste. My heart was racing, blood thundered in my ears. Uncertain of what to expect, other than death, I clenched my fist and waited for swift retribution. As moments passed, deep in the fog of my mind it registered that I remained alive and nothing had changed. The insect percussion continued undisturbed.

Perhaps I had not touched it long enough to induce death—only injury? The skin on my palm was pink and tender from the scrape, but otherwise unblemished.

He watched my reaction, waiting for me to acknowledge his truth, knowing doubt was taking root. If Adam was wrong about the tree, where else was he mistaken? I reached out and touched the tree of my own volition, resting my fingers against the cool, gnarled bark. It was strong beneath my hand, steady. So conditioned was I for male approval, I turned to Lucifer, and responded to his nod with a smile. Something shifted within me as that seed began to sprout.

'Adam is a liar and a fool,' he said.

I turned my head. I couldn't bear to think of him as either. What did that make me?

Lucifer plucked a leaf from the tree and brushed it against my arm. Emboldened by his action, I caressed the leaf's glossy smoothness. No pain nor distress befell me. Rather, I felt intoxicated; I knew something Adam didn't. Giddy with this knowledge, I realized my transgression, my unfettered disobedience, and I cast about to see if I'd been caught. There was no change in the birdsong, no change in the sky. I felt relieved.

Intent on my every reaction, Lucifer bore witness to my deed with encouragement in his eyes. A static charge filled the air, this shared secret forming a bond between us. I turned my face to his, my lips parted as I drew breath. We stood on the brink of something.

'The fruit is the best part.' His whisper was hypnotizing in its resonance. A simple statement that drew my eyes to the clustered orbs.

Lucifer plucked a rosy globe and rubbed it against his naked thigh. He lifted it to his mouth and bit into the flesh, never taking his eyes from mine. His eyelids half closed as if in ecstasy. His lips glistened as he ate, plump lips, moist with nectar. My pulse beat faster at the aroma of musk which filled the air, his scent and the fruit's, making my skin flush and my mouth dry. And the jungle fell silent, for I heard only the sound of him, the crunch of his white teeth sinking into the yielding flesh, the lick of his tongue around his lips, the swallow of his throat.

Lucifer smiled and held out the fruit for me to taste. It looked so delicious and not poisonous at all. I yearned to please Lucifer, to share in this tasting, but Adam's fear stopped me. With great effort, I shook my head and stepped back.

'Why did God tell Adam about this tree and its fruit if he didn't intend for you to partake?'

'Adam says it is a test of obedience.'

'Obedience to what? A lie? You know the truth. What is the value of a pointless test?'

'To test our faith.'

'Should you place your faith in a lie?'

'Adam says...'

'I didn't ask for Adam's opinion.'

No one ever asked for my thoughts. I had never pondered such questions before. My life was ordered and controlled according to Adam's agenda. It was a new sensation to speak my mind. 'I think He must have a reason for lying.'

Lucifer gave me such a smile of approval, I basked in its glow. He moved closer, so close, the hair on his chest brushed my skin.

'So you believe God a liar.'

I began to protest that he misunderstood my words, but he pressed his fingers to my lips.

'For what reason? He puts risk before you and gives you choices. He seeks to test your courage and your ingenuity, not your obedience.'

'I don't know—'

'Did He plant this tree in isolation? Birds sit in its branches. Bees pollinate the fruit. No other creature avoids it. Why should you?'

Lucifer brought his hand with the fruit close to my mouth. His fingers brushed against my lips and a tingle passed through my body filling me with longing.

'It won't harm me?' Its spicy sweetness made my mouth watered.

I trusted his gentle nod, leaned forward and took a bite from the fruit in his outstretched hand. It yielded to my teeth with soft surrender and my mouth filled with luscious flesh and sweet ambrosia. The pleasure of that one bite reverberated throughout my whole body and I craved more. I bit again, unable to take enough into my mouth. My lips brushed against his sticky sweet fingers, and I licked them. I heard his soft laugh as he offered them to me and his gasp as I took one into my mouth and sucked it clean. Pleasure rippled from mouth to breast to groin and I groaned and writhed, unable to stop.

His eyes changed. I saw a small flash of something like triumph, gone before I could be certain.

Lucifer cupped my hands around the rest of the fruit.

'You're full of surprises, Eve.'

I'd have devoured the whole of that sweet treat right then, but he stopped me.

'The pleasure is greater when shared by two. Take the rest to Adam.'

With that, he vanished and with him the light in this darkest part of the garden dimmed. I felt the loss so deep, I placed a hand against the tree. The warm bark reassured me. The pulse within the tree strengthened me. I don't remember how long I stood there but when I regained my senses, dusk was upon me.

I looked at the half-eaten fruit in my hands. I didn't want to share with Adam what I had shared with Lucifer and had no hesitation in eating the rest of the fruit myself. I ran my tongue over the imprint of his teeth, hoping to taste him too. Each mouthful brought me pleasure but lacked intensity without his presence. I gulped mouthfuls, hoping for a return of those powerful sensations but the enchantment waned.

To hide my gluttony, I picked another globe from the tree, and from that, I took a single bite. I chose poorly. Although red and shiny outside, the pale flesh was grainy, without the scent and succulence of Lucifer's choice. I spat out the offending chunk and contemplated picking another fruit, without the same enthusiasm.

With my flawed bounty, I ran through the darkening forest, ignoring the deafening song and the scratch of branches. I tripped over roots, grazing my elbows and knees on rough bark, without loosening my grip on my prize.

I returned to the glade where Adam and I slept, hoping the fading light might hide my disheveled state

'Where have you been?' Adam's voice reproached me from the gloom. 'I've been waiting and I'm hungry.'

I gave him the fruit I'd picked and sat beside him on the grass.

'You've already had a bite!' he said.

'Only a little one,' I soothed. I wrapped my hands around his, and the fruit, mimicking Lucifer, and waggled it close to Adam's lips urging him in soft tones to take a bite.

Adam snatched free from my hands. He bit into the flesh and tore a mouthful, chewing loudly. I heard him swallow and watched the morsel pass down his throat.

'I don't recognize the taste. Where did you get it?'

I didn't know how to reply. A hundred possible answers flashed through my mind.

'Which tree, Eve?' Adam put down the fruit and peered at me.

'You know,' I said.

His eyes grew wide and his face pale. He made a retching sound and I thought he was going to vomit.

'Why did you do this to me?' he gasped.

I kept silent. I didn't know how to express the ecstasy I'd felt when Lucifer fed me the fruit. How this afternoon had awakened a sense of worth, and how my first act of disobedience thrilled me. I'd hoped Adam would feel the same.

He slapped me across the face, knocking me to the ground.

'Are you too stupid to do as you're told?'

I drew my knees to my chest and waited.

'He knows what you've done. What you made me do! You've put me in a terrible position. I'll have to go and tell him you're sorry. That you'll make amends.'

He left to commune with God and I lay in the darkness. I wished he'd invited me to go as well. Just once it would be nice to hear the Word of God firsthand. I heard the chirp of crickets and the rustle of something moving in the undergrowth. The comfort of small familiar things. I wondered if He did know, why had He not stopped me before I pulled Adam into my deceit? Perhaps Lucifer was right: it was all some sort of test and I had failed.

I must have fallen asleep for the next thing I knew was Adam shaking me. The sky behind him was a pale grey and I couldn't see his face properly.

'It's time to go, Eve.' His voice was low and harsh. Beyond the anger he'd shown last night.

I sat up and rubbed my eyes. 'Go where?'

He didn't answer. He turned away and started walking. I scrambled to my feet and ran after him. He strode with purpose, his long legs taking steps twice the length of mine. There were tears falling from his eyes. My heart constricted in my breast and I felt more frightened than I had in the dark forest with Lucifer.

'What did He say, Adam?'

He didn't slow his steps and his words were punctuated with deep breaths and choking sobs. 'He gave me a choice. Leave with you or stay here alone. You have spoiled everything!'

'What does that mean?' I was running and crying too, not understanding his explanation.

Up ahead, I saw Uriel standing at the edge of Eden, his flaming sword held high above his head. He was waiting for me. Adam had chosen to cast me out. I stopped running.

'No!' I cried. 'Punish me any way but not that!'

Adam grabbed my arm and pulled me close. His lips were drawn back in a grimace, spittle-flecked at the corners. His eyes were wide and wild. 'You've punished us both by your reckless disobedience. He won't forgive you and I cannot.'

'I'm sorry. I know it was wrong.' I said the words although I didn't mean them. I'd never seen him so angry and it frightened me. 'What can I do to make things right?'

'There is nothing, Eve. Why couldn't you do as you were told?'

'I will. I promise.'

He looked at me, a snarl on his lips. 'You won't survive a day out there without me.'

I knelt on the ground and kissed his feet. 'Then don't send me. I will never disobey you again. Please, Adam.'

'It's too late.'

Adam grabbed my arm and dragged me towards Uriel. My pleas and struggles were insufficient against his anger-fueled strength. I went limp against the ground. Adam picked me up, swung me over his shoulder and carried me out of Eden.

He kept walking. I twisted my head and saw Uriel growing smaller in the distance. I had not expected this. I, like Adam, expected God to punish me, not us both. But Adam chose to go with me rather than remain companionless in Eden. My action exposed Adam's greatest fear: the prospect of being alone.

Adam's loyalty to me became a yoke about my neck. God set us free from Eden, and Adam bound me to him. He blamed me for his predicament. I should have challenged him. And challenged Him. Blamed Lucifer. But guilt stopped me. Guilt at the frisson of pleasure that rippled through my body whenever I thought about that afternoon with Lucifer.

I had thought myself content before our encounter but I'd known no different. My life had been preordained. I was obedient in all matters. A tiny spark of rebellion caught alight that day, and I nursed and fanned it since.

In the years that followed, we discovered a far greater consequence of my disobedience than banishment. I learned over time that the Ancient Egyptians called that tree the Tree of Life and Death. Others also knew of the tree: in Taoist belief, Norse mythology, and Arabic tradition it is the Tree of Immortality. My actions that day affected Adam and me for eternity, and everyone else.

God forbade us from eating from that tree not as a test, but as a gift. By eating its bounty, I robbed us of the gift God bestowed upon us; His gift of senescence, the ability to age and die. The ability to experience fleeting life with wonder. With a single bite, I doomed us to athanasia—unending agelessness and lifetimes of repeated lessons. My action overturned God's choice and took in its stead, Lucifer's. This was the first time I was a pawn in their battle.

That recollection of the taste and texture of that fruit, of Lucifer's fingers, still thrills me but is tinged with regret. He knew what he was doing when he stirred the hornet's nest of longing within me. The temptation he laid at my feet opened my eyes to choice, to independent thought and action, and showed me how different life could be. He sealed my fate and mapped the future of humankind.

I regret my impulsiveness every day I spend in exile. Not for the freedoms it brought me—those I cherish—but for the stain upon my name and for the manner in which things unfolded. The consequences of my actions were too far-reaching, infecting humanity, turning men distrustful, and shaming women. The cloud I cast over humanity brings the acid reign of free will, if one is brave enough to hold out a hand and catch the drops as they fall.

The sound of the motorboat engine changes as we approach the dock. The captain maneuvers us closer to the bollards with short bursts of power. As we bob back and forth, I wonder again what Lucifer's motivations are in offering me this prize. I now know Lucifer does nothing without self-gain. No longer the wide-eyed innocent, I am not so swayed by the promise of perfect fruit.

4

BLASPHEMY

Adam chose Eve, because there was no other.
Musæus, *Volksmärchen der Deutschen*, III, 219

Lucifer awaits my response. I laugh. The idea is preposterous.

'You can't give me Eden.'
'Why not?'
'It's not yours to give.'
'Not His fabrication. Mine.'
I am confused.
'How do you envision Eden—as it was back then? The Flood destroyed most of it and war the rest. Your Eden is long gone, but if God can recreate it for you, so can I. There's no copyright on landscaping.'

I'd imagined Eden frozen in time, the idyll unchanged over the millennia. No details were specified in my negotiations with God, and Lucifer's revelation saddens me. Trees grow, streams dwindle, animals die. Yet, it is more than geography I long for, it's the simplicity of life without hardship. An end to loneliness and a return to joy. Oblivion.

'Is that possible?' I take the bait.

That gleam in his eyes—he's ready to reel me in. 'Give up tonight's battle. Break your contract with God. Bind to me and you shall receive.'

'Exactly as I remember it?'

There is a loud crack behind me. Paving stones at the center of St. Mark's Square fracture, pushed aside and upward as a giant stalk fights its way through. One by one the shop front windows in the cloistered walkway shatter spraying splinters of glass in all directions. Columns crumble. Steps catapult into the air, propelled by more rising stems thickening as they shoot skyward.

The bell tower implodes and sinks to the ground. A gaping hole in the center of the square. Water gushes from below filling it in minutes. The air is ripped apart by screams. Bodies topple over balconied edges, spew out of buildings. Wailing rends the air as a wave of bodies expels from the cathedral with other flying debris. They land with sickening thuds against the marble flagstones. All civility is lost as stragglers scramble over each other, desperate to escape. The lucky ones kick and push their way through the chaos, sharing simple goals; to avoid the falling masonry and being trampled by each other. And amidst the destruction, nature grows at lightning speed. Twisting and thrusting, I can almost hear the leaves gasping for air as they sprout forth. They remind me to breathe.

'Is this an illusion?'

'Reality, Eve.' He plucks daisies from the grass at our feet, splits a stem to make a chain. 'As real as you and me.'

The smell of ozone fills the air and there is a tang of blood and bone, as the garden feeds on the dead. I no longer hear the cries of tourists, only the creaking growth spurts of plants as they reclaim civilization. Humanity makes the ultimate sacrifice for me—as I brought pain to humankind when I left Eden, so I am required to inflict it again to gain my prize.

The Grand Canal dwindles to a tumbling river, its bridges fallen into the sparkling water. The waterside palaces are replaced by trees with low hanging fruit and bramble vines heavy with blue and purple clusters. I spy the little path I walked each day to bathe in the stream. The smell of orange blossom and jasmine is overwhelming and under my feet soft springy meadow grasses push their way through the forgotten jewels. The same kingfisher hovers above the river.

'What about Venice?'

He shrugs. 'It was sinking anyway.'

'And the people?'

'Recycled.'

'Murdered!'

He shrugs, looks across the canal and tosses his head in the direction of the Basilica di Santa Maria della Salute. 'Never my favorite place. All that pious Redentore stuff makes me uneasy.'

'Maybe you shouldn't have sent them the plague for so long.'

He grins. 'I just do as I'm told.'

'Is this a preview or the real thing?'

'It's whatever you want, Eve.'

The garden grows around us gaining maturity and beyond the ruined cathedral, I can see the top of a tree rising with alacrity, shiny green leaves dotted with red fruit and snow white blossom, its branches spreading wide. My mouth waters at the memory. Lucifer squeezes my hand.

He remembers too. It smells like Eden: the earth after rain, herbs crushed underfoot, the ripeness of fruit and flower.

It is the heartsease for which I have searched. I want to kick off my shoes, tear the dress from my body and run to the stream. I try to block out the rumble of nature digging and clawing its way through grand façades and humble homes. It wounds me deeply that a city and its people are dying to satisfy my whim. Because of me. Again. Gondolas smash against the piers and are dragged beneath churning waves until only their staffed prows remain as markers of their watery graves.

The ground shudders as every trace of Venice washes away.

My breath comes fast and tight, conflicting and gasping within my chest as I stifle my sobs.

'So much death,' I whisper.

He crushes my hand in his. 'I would destroy the whole world if you asked me to.'

'It's wrong.'

'Says you who dispenses death to thousands at my gates.'

'Not the same.'

'Ah, yes. It's all right when it's done in God's name.' The bitterness in his voice strikes a chord.

'Stop!'

He turns brimstone eyes to me and laughs. 'Why should I?'

Consumed by light, his hair ablaze, his magnificence and malevolence dwarf all else. His indifference to the plight of Venice and its inhabitants is clear. Humanity is insignificant in his scheme of things. Worse. He is jealous of humanity, of my commitment to preserving it. He knows guilt haunts me at the misery I have caused so many. Because of me, misogyny has flourished unchecked. I am the convenient truth that allowed women to be vilified, burned and disempowered over the ages. My story has been the blade wielded against feminine power. I cannot allow further destruction to happen in my name.

'Please,' I beg. 'If you stop, I promise to consider your offer.' I expect him to laugh off my words, but he cocks his head, his expression terse and inscrutable. The fate of so many lies in that gesture.

'Please.'

The clench of his jaw softens and he waves his hand.

The transformation stops, swallows itself like a snake eating its tail. Nature relinquishes her grip and retreats beneath the cold marble tiles, tamed back into mosaic splendor. Grass shrivels, birdsong fades. Venice reassembles.

People rise and look around in bewilderment before resuming their sightseeing as the hands on a clock turn anticlockwise in some dusty attic. The queue in front of the cathedral pops up like a row of dominoes in reverse motion. Rising from the rubble in a cloud of dust, St. Mark's clocktower resumes its vigil and the Moors strike the bells, announcing the hour.

'How has it gotten so late? We should get back to the hotel.' A girl in a baseball cap links arms with a tall boy. A family with ice creams wanders past a tour guide with an umbrella herding a flock of hatted tourists.

'Thank you,' I say.

'No humans were hurt in the making.' He purses his lips. 'So, what's your answer?'

'I promised to consider, so give me some time.'

I glimpse regret in his expression before he hides behind

his mask of indifference. 'What's there to think about? You want it or not?'

This is what I have dreamed of, fought for, and prayed for, for so long. Here it is. Offered with thirty pieces of silver. An escape from my earthly existence.

'You wouldn't "need time" if He offered,' he sneers. 'What keeps you bound, Eve?'

I am frightened he'll guess the truth. He knows me well enough to work it out. Eden is my dream, but the other is my secret obsession. An obsession I have to abandon once I enter Eden.

'God's Eden brings forgiveness. Yours comes with guilt.'

'What if mine is the only Eden you can have? Be honest, what good is Eden without me in it? Make a choice. You have until midnight to give me your answer.'

His words cut deep. Millennia of waiting. He voices my worst fear.

§

BACK IN THE JUNKYARD, I inhale the dry desert dust instead of the brine of Venice. Still reeling from his remarks and the dizzy transition, it takes me a moment to orient myself. By the play of shadows, I realize I am returned to the exact second of our departure with only a few moments of day left. He wants me to think him honorable in our negotiations.

Alone by the ashes, no glass slipper in sight, I stand before the pyre in my jeans, boots and ponytail. With shaking hands, I reach into my pocket for my nicotine crutch. Cigarette in hand, a vision in dinginess, I inhale strength and push Lucifer from my mind. A few puffs and I'm focused on my final fight. I toss the spent butt onto the waiting logs. This time there is no alchemy to prevent the diesel from catching alight. I take a burning stick from the flames and thrust it deep into the pyre, add my breath to give it force, to ensure it burns fierce and even.

That half-breath between day and night shrinks against my bonfire. You might think fire against demons is an exercise in futility: Hell is a torment-filled inferno with conflagrations designed for never-ending torture. Those red and green flames leave no mark on the bodies of the damned, while the oxygen-fueled tongues of this orange and blue can lick a demon's flesh from its bones. I ready for my final battle as Samhain begins.

My fire casts grotesque shadows that dance upon the graffitied wall in a parody of the painted mural. The wall transforms. It expands beyond all semblance of earthly proportion and the images on it warp.

I am struck by the enormity of this barrier between Earth and beyond. Dark as granite, dull as clay, it soars above the junkyard. Gates form directly before me: two gigantic plates of unholy metal glowing red hot. Fused together. A malevolent wind stirs, bringing the stench of desperation.

No other place smells as bad. There's none of the fire or brimstone that preachers boast about (that I'd welcome as a fresh breeze). This odor of Hell comes from a cesspit of cruelty. I force myself to breathe it in. This is the fragrance of my road to salvation.

Worse than the stench, is the terror that emanates from this liminal barrier. A taste of Hell's power that seeps through. That fell arcana stretches to my bonfire, catches twig and flame within its spell. My backyard blaze expands into a holocaust capable of razing a city. The ground shudders and, with a grinding wail, Hell's Gates bulge outward, the press of Lucifer's forces eager to be unleashed. Slowly those fiery plates tear apart, jagged and raw—flesh split open, the edges cauterized by hellfire. Beyond that bleeding gash between worlds, within the Acherontic void, my uncountable foe awaits.

5

HERESY

The true soldier fights not because he hates what is in front
of him, but because he loves what is behind him.
G. K. Chesterton, *ILN*, 1/14/1911

MY SWORD SLIPS FROM ITS SHEATH WITH A WHISPER. The runes etched along the blade glimmer with anticipation as I adjust my grip. I am ready to face the demon host. Again. Here to perform my penance: to engage in a battle I detest, to wipe away my Original Sin.

At first, the only sound is the crackle of my fire, but now, drums beat from afar. An eerie screeching starts. It's always a shock as the first tranche of warriors spew forth through the torn gates, eyes blinking as they adjust from the underworld gloom. They come in all shapes and sizes, hooved and winged. Tusks jut from twisted mouths, beady-eyes beneath boney-ridged brows. The frontrunners are the weak and puny but each is still larger than me. Those that stop, mesmerized by the bonfire, are trampled under the host that swells behind them.

They fill every inch of the space between Hell and my

bonfire, shoulder to shoulder, and snarl at me. I stand, one against many, and assess their mood. Frenzy palpates the air. Young and inexperienced demons, unable to control their enthusiasm, break formation and dash towards the bonfire. Their sergeants leap after them and cut them down. Lucifer demands total obedience even in his absence. The executions quiet the front ranks, but the rest of the horde fidgets and squabbles, growing impatient.

The spectacle begins. Claws rasp against taut leathery hides, hooves pound the ground. Grunting and barking, they roll their eyes until all I see are yellowy whites. Lips pull back into bloodless maws, tongues thrust like daggers. Hooves and wings beat a savage tune and horns clash together.

Some gyrate their hips in gestures rude and violent. Others hurl insults and stones through the flames. My pulse races. It doesn't matter how many times I've seen this dance. It still terrifies me.

The drums and screeching stops. Demons quiet—responding to a silent command. As one, the army surges forward. Force from the rear lifts the first platoon, pushing them onto the pyre where they turn into living torches, howling and screaming, trying to escape the inexorable wave that swells forward and down.

The blue beech remains impervious to this attempt to smother its flames. Instead, the fire catches. The air fills with the sweet odor of demon flesh. Delicate and reminiscent of roasting chestnuts and toffee, this delicious aroma purifies the hellstench. My bonfire reaches gargantuan proportion with the addition of demon fuel. My choice of blue beech proves justified.

There is no mourning of their fallen as the next ranks move into place to reinforce the flesh wall. Lucifer's generals prowl the length of their troops, keeping discipline, but despite their presence, hundreds of spats erupt. More than usual. Another silent command. The demon host turn and a pathway opens in its midst.

Down the swathe cut through Lucifer's forces comes a pale procession. The souls of the newly dead. The thinning of the liminal veil on Samhain allows these souls who are in limbo one last kindness—a night back on Earth to attend to unfinished business. One night to say goodbyes to their loved ones. They will return at dawn and once behind those fiery gates, they must accept their final judgement, be it a ticket to hell or otherwise.

And, demons will take advantage of any opportunity to slip into the mortal world. They yearn for a night of debauchery and the chance to pervert humans in a myriad of ways, and try to secret themselves amongst the human host.

As the spectral exodus drifts into the night, I watch for interlopers. Demons skulk in the shadows, hoping to pass unnoticed. Those with the ability to shapeshift assume human forms. The bold believe they can outrun or outfight me. Whatever their tactic, their evil gives them away. There is no way to hide the despair that seeps from them, that dark emanation that oozes terror.

Tonight, the first to try is a shifter assuming the human form of a frail old woman. Its aura leaks black with each step. It shuffles left and right, weaving through the column of departing souls. In its eagerness to escape it moves too quickly, overtaking the other souls.

'Turn back,' I warn.

They never do, but I offer the chance. It screams and lunges, reality pulsing through the charade. One moment I see a wizened old face, the next a grotesque mask. I wince as

I cut the old woman's head from her shoulders. It rolls, lopsided, resuming its true form with each rotation, beaked and leathery until it comes to a halt.

'Poor Gary.' Lucifer says, making an appearance in black; jeans and V-neck sweater, expensive but understated. 'The first of your many victims tonight, no doubt.' He performs a mock benediction over the fallen demon and head and body disappear. The demon wall roars.

'They're angry tonight.' I scan the procession.

'It's hard to watch your brethren die,' Lucifer says.

'But easy to walk over them.'

'What choice do you give them? Clear the way so they can walk around.'

I ignore him and cut down another escaping demon. Lucifer waves his arm at his assembled minions.

'You slaughter my children. I knew each by name. That's far worse than the anonymous tourists I culled in Venice. Come on, Evie, it's your last gig. Show a little compassion.'

'I'm not the villain here. I'm just performing my penance.'

To him, penance is a dirty word. 'Ever wonder why He likes penitents on their knees?' He thrusts his hips forward and licks his lips.

'You know He'll never let you go. You've done your job too well, gatekeeper.'

Uneasiness grips me and latches onto Lucifer's words. I've shown up every Samhain without fail, not a sick day in two thousand years. Humans sleep easier because of me. God needs another champion in my stead. The thought fills me with dread. I have stayed too long. My mistake was making myself indispensable, instead of rendering my task obsolete. Lucifer delights at pointing out my error, but I must trust in God's plan.

'He promised.'

Belly laughter erupts from him.

'What incentive does he have to grant your wish now? He has airport security at both terminals. You at Hell's gate, and my brother Uriel at Heaven's.'

He's a master at obfuscating the greys of right and wrong, but his argument has a more practical purpose. The wall of demons moves forward, testing the edge of the bonfire and several figures dart in and out of the soul caravan, to sneak past while he distracts me.

'Nice try.' I turn away from him and face the demons.

'Oh, Eve, how did we manage before you came along?' A single graceful leap puts him high on a stack of tires. 'Do His dirty work, play Hercules to his Atlas. Isn't banishment for eternity enough? I say again, there is no release if you follow His path. I, on the other hand... tick-tock.'

I shouldn't let him goad me. I shiver and strike out, cutting left and right, keeping me from having to answer. There is a flurry of tusks and horns as two demons charge, hoping to barge their way through. One succeeds, the other takes my sword through its neck. I place my foot on the demon's chest and pull my sword free.

He calls down from his perch. 'Let God tell you what to do, what to think, who to kill, who to love.'

'It's not that easy,' I say. 'There are other considerations.'

'Such as Adam in your Eden to make it complete?'

I blink and miss a demon with my blade.

Adam never figures in my plans. In my daydreams, Eden is that afternoon by the river. With Lucifer. But his banishment from Eden is more binding than mine.

'You still love Adam.' His pout and sulky tone amuse me. I know his demeanor is contrived, but there is some small satisfaction in imagining Lucifer jealous.

'He is my husband.' Why did I say that? I don't want any misunderstanding where Adam is concerned.

Lucifer laughs. 'A little late to play the faithful card, Eve. Perhaps it's Adam's forgiveness you seek more than God's?'

I lunge to my right and stab at more demons, turning so Lucifer can't see the heat that suffuses my cheeks. A jab to the left and I bring down a small demon disguised as a child. Perhaps I have been too willing to let others decide my fate.

'I want nothing from Adam.'

'What is your unfinished business, Evie?'

My unfinished business is not with Adam. Adam and I finished centuries ago. But Lucifer is right, I've lingered here for another reason. Cain.

The day God cursed Cain to wander endlessly, unable to be killed by another, he cursed me too. I know my son is somewhere on Earth. I just don't know where, although I've looked.

I am afraid to admit how much I long to see him. This is the son that I was told to turn away from. I yearn for a single glimpse of his face. Perhaps to touch his hand, or kiss his cheek one more time. Buried so deep inside me, this secret is a tumor in my belly. It is my weakness and Lucifer would exploit it if he guessed at the truth.

'There's nothing.'

'So you say.' His smile is disbelieving. 'There's a reason you wear this battle like a hairshirt, year after year. If not for Adam, then for whom?'

He mustn't guess.

I twist to avoid a blow and stumble as a claw grazes my

shoulder. My hands are sweating and the hilt of my sword slips from my grasp. I pick up a burning branch from the fire and hurl it at a cluster of demons. They run on, unperturbed.

'Go to Hell,' I say.

'Come join me.' He smirks. 'It's lovely there this time of year.'

Lucifer walks through the flames and stands with his generals.

6

IDOLATRY

> The pleasure of love lasts only a moment,
> The grief of love lasts a lifetime.
> Jean-Pierre Claris de Florian, *Plaisir d'amour*

CAIN DAZZLED ME FROM THE MOMENT I FIRST HELD him in my arms. I marveled at his tiny perfection, his fingers, his toes, the softness of his new skin. The suck of his mouth pulling at my breast, his fist curled against my swollen flesh. I held him close as he slept and listened to him breathe, every snuffle and burp a joy to hear. He was my gift from God, a lessening of the blow of banishment. And he needed me. Only me. Not Adam.

My days were spent in my garden with Cain. I was proud of what I managed to achieve by taming a small square of wilderness. I dug deep to find fertile soil and deeper still to find water. On my walks, I gathered seedlings, took cuttings from bushes and trees, and dug up tender shoots with my nails and bits of bone. I tilled the ground, planted and watered my garden with care. A pale imitation of Eden, but it was mine.

As the seasons passed and Cain grew, I realized God had blessed Cain with a gift. Under his chubby toddler fingers, the spindliest stalks grew straight and tall. Fruit swelled and ripened regardless of drought or flood. At the sound of his voice, flowers turned their heads.

Also, God filled him with respect for the life of all creatures. Cain refused to kill, whether for sport, for food or offering. No flesh of any animal we slaughtered passed his lips. He ate only what the ground yielded. When nuts and berries grew scarce in winter, and the ground became too hard to dig for tubers, I would ration out what was left of our dried stores, saving the best for him. But as winter dragged on and our stores were emptied, Cain weakened and took to his bed.

I begged him to eat some dried meat, held a bowl of bone broth to his lips. But despite my tears and cajoling, he always turned his lips away.

'It's not in my nature,' he said.

I thought that strange. Wasn't he the same as us?

'Is it in your nature to die?' I wept.

'It is not,' he reassured me, and he was right. When spring returned, he too blossomed to vibrant health, as lush and plump as fruit on a tree.

My love for Cain didn't go unnoticed. For every tenderness I bestowed on him, Adam dealt a blow. At first, he was surreptitious in his punishments, a little harsher than he needed to be. But soon, I would notice Cain limping, or wincing when I hugged him. He never complained, but I saw the bruises and grew colder towards Adam. I pretended sleep when he came to me at night. It didn't stop him from waking me to take his pleasure. Our contempt for each other grew swift weeds in our relationship and neither of us stopped to pluck them.

It pleased me when Adam began to wander further from our home, spending days on end in the wilderness. His absence allowed me time alone with Cain without worrying about the consequences. When he returned from these trips he was changed. He spoke with excitement about tribes he'd found beyond the desert. He brought gifts; skins of their fermented grain drink and foods made from cooked milk. They welcomed him and he wanted me to return with him and live with them. I refused. I had my garden and my son and wanted nothing more.

'I'll go without you!' he shouted. 'I'll have a new life with women who appreciate me, not treat me with scorn.'

Adam drank the fermented drink and his mood changed. He grabbed me about the neck and screamed at me, his breath pungent, his eyes wild. He threw me to the ground and kicked me. I didn't recognize him and I didn't recognize myself. I didn't fight him or defend myself; I became passive. That made him angrier and rougher. He pulled my hair, twisted my arms, longing for the reaction I denied him. He boasted about the wild women he'd lain with at the tribes, how they painted their bodies and used their mouths. He wondered aloud why I didn't moan with the enthusiasm they did.

I endured his outbursts for several nights—until the skins ran dry—until he gathered his things and headed back across the desert. When he returned months later, he could see I was again with child.

Abel had Adam's looks and Adam's affection. His birth stopped Adam's travels and forced us to live as a family. It wasn't all bad—I enjoyed having another pair of hands to help with the work.

I found Abel slow and clumsy. He cried and fed slowly, and I resented that he took me from my garden and Cain. I weaned him early to sheep's milk and Adam fashioned a sling and carried him to the grazing pasture during the days. He taught Abel to walk and talk, and when he was old enough, to hunt and fish and tend the livestock.

When Abel grew hair on his chin, Adam spoke of taking our sons across the desert to find them wives. I made excuses, finding reasons why they could not leave yet. The harvests, the lambing, the weather. But I knew the day would come soon when I could no longer hold them back.

Cain laughed and wrapped his arms about me. 'It would take more than a wife to drive me from you,' he said. To prove his devotion, he worked tirelessly in our garden. From the stories I'd told him of Eden, he planned and planted another that stretched from my doorstep to the sunset.

Too soon our sons reached manhood, yet Adam and I stayed as we were. It was impossible to tell parent from child and this bothered Abel greatly.

'What is the secret to never growing old?' he asked.

'Betrayal,' Adam replied. 'May your wives never bestow it upon you.'

7

PERJURY

The function of prayer is not to influence God, but rather to
change the nature of the one who prays.
Søren Kierkegaard

IT WAS OUR CUSTOM TO OFFER A SACRIFICE AT THE END
of the season to thank God for our harvests and livestock. I
woke my sons before dawn to begin our preparations. Abel
took a strong newborn lamb, bleating for its mother, and tied
its legs together. He threw the shivering thing over his
shoulder and headed to our altar in time for sunrise. Cain
went into the fields to choose his offering. He took so long
that Abel, impatient to be done, made his sacrifice alone.

'You kept God waiting,' Abel said when Cain arrived at
the altar.

'The better to serve him,' Cain said. As the altar was
sticky with lamb's blood and smoking lamb fat, Cain placed
his single gourd on the ground below.

'Must God bend so low to receive such little due?'
Adam kicked the gourd away.

The sky grew dark and a cold wind blew. Vultures

appeared overhead, circling silently. There was fear in Adam's eyes. He grabbed Cain by the scruff of his shirt and threw him to the ground.

'You bring displeasure upon us all. Go back into the fields. Take your brother and find a more suitable bounty. The most precious gift you can present to God. One that will not incur His wrath upon this house.'

I said nothing. My eyes pleaded with Cain not to make matters worse, as he and Adam were equally stubborn. I collected the discarded gourd and placed it on the altar before returning home to my chores. I was spinning flax when I heard Adam's wails and I rushed outside. He approached me, bearing the body of Abel in his arms. At first I thought he'd been attacked by a wild beast. I ran to them and when I drew close, I saw the gash across Abel's neck, a slice clean and deep, the stroke made by a sacrificial blade.

'Your son has slain my son!' Adam wept.

'That's not possible,' I said. 'Cain walks lightly to avoid crushing ants. How can you accuse him of such a thing?' I rushed away to find Cain.

He was kneeling in the wheatfields, on bloodied ground, his expression blank.

'What happened here? Tell me your father is mistaken.' My voice was not my own.

'I did as I was bid,' Cain said.

I couldn't believe what I was hearing. 'Are you saying he's right?'

'He instructed me to bring the thing I held most precious.'

The world was spinning around me. I clutched at Cain's shoulder to steady myself.

'You blame your father for this? It is you who has

broken my heart! I labored to bring you both into this world. What right had you to take him from me?'

Cain looked up at me, his eyes large saucers of emptiness.

'Surely he belonged to God more than you? He was God-given, and is now God given. All those lambs you sacrifice in a year—this is no different. Those lambs had mothers too.'

I threw myself at him, screaming and slapping and punching until my fists were bruised, my throat horse, my mouth stretched in a silent scream.

He did nothing to stop me. I hit him upon his back and shoulders, slapped his face. He stayed silent, as he did with Adam, and that made me stop. Sobbing, I sank to the ground beside him, staring at him, begging him with my eyes to explain. I grabbed his bloodstained hands and tried to scrub them clean with the hem of my skirt. He pulled free from me and walked away leaving me crying amidst the wheat.

Adam took Abel's body into the hills and spoke with God. When he returned, alone, he was calmed. I washed Abel's body and dressed him in his best shirt. Bathed him with cool water and my tears. Adam and I sat in silence and waited for Cain.

It was dark when he returned. Adam spoke the words God told him to say:

'No longer will the ground, that you have soaked with your brother's blood, respond to your touch. No seed you plant shall flourish. You will stray from place to place, unable to find solace as you ponder your deed. You shall bear my mark, so none may rob you of your punishment with the gift of death.'

Cain stood quietly, his face in shadow, and I could not

read him. One look from him and I would have pleaded with Adam and God for clemency. His silence filled my heart with sorrow equal to the pain of losing Abel.

The mark of Cain. It settled about him, a miasma of ruthlessness. A soul-deep warning to keep away. An aura of repulsion that made my skin itch.

'Leave and never return.' Adam, his voice full of anger and quiet venom, turned his back on our son. I opened my mouth but no sound would leave. Cain laughed, a mirthless guffaw, and walked away.

I stumbled to our bed, exhausted with grief and disbelief, and slept fitfully, my dreams filled with blood and screams. I don't know where Adam went to assuage his grief but I woke to grim morning cold and alone. My world had ended. Again.

My beautiful son, who never killed a living thing before, unrecognizable to me by his deed. I tried to go after him, but Adam forbade me. He stood in the doorway and blocked my passage, impervious to my pleas and tears. It was a punishment too cruel. I had lost one son and now the other was taken. Cain, like me, doomed to immortality for his sin.

I withdrew. As I always did. I accepted the judgement meted out by Adam, interpreted by Adam, although my soul cried that it was wrong. I was ashamed by Cain's actions. There was a fear, deep inside, that in some way I had contributed to Cain's behavior—was he flawed like me? And beside shame sat guilt: how had I allowed so harsh a punishment to be inflicted without considering all arguments?

Adam became more zealous in his devotions. 'Blind faith,' he said. 'It is not for us to understand, only to obey. It will bring you peace.' I didn't want peace; I wanted understanding. I'd heard that platitude before and Lucifer had dispelled that illusion.

I no longer wanted to trust in God. He had taken both my sons. My obedience was only an apathy for which I despised myself. I returned to lay listless on my bed, my face swollen and red. Filled with self-pity, I refused to rise.

Adam towered over me.

'Goodbye, Eve.' There was nothing but defeat in his voice. I turned my head away from him, not caring.

I heard him lift his pack onto his back, the dull clatter as he collected his spears and walking stick. His feet on the leaves outside my door.

IT WAS the first time I tried to die. I stopped eating and drinking, and although I grew thin and weak, I remained alive. Too weak to stand, I lay on the cold earth of my hut hoping for death to come, yet I was denied that release. I knew the gnawing pain of starvation and delirium. I lost track of time, and of the distinction between waking and sleep, of reality and dream.

Many times, I imagined myself back in the Garden, sitting by the river, watching the birds and butterflies. I woke once and there were daisies wilted on the floor beside me. Perhaps that too was a dream. Too weak to open my eyes, everything was a dream.

Often my mouth filled with the taste of fruit. Sweet and juicy, it sustained me and I would cry and try to spit it out. I cursed, screamed abuse at my rescuer. Begged him to let me fade away to nothing, but he remained stalwart. I felt his comfort even as I was on the brink of madness. I know not who my savior was—God or Lucifer.

After so long alone, I woke one morning aware of another's presence. Adam returned to visit me. I saw in his eyes his shock at my appearance. I must have looked bad, for he put down his pack and stayed for a while. He helped me bathe and wash and comb my hair. He cooked me bone broth and picked the last of the season's berries from our brambles.

I found him changed by our loss too. There was a madness about him, a slyness in his expression. He was secretive and withdrawn and refused to talk about where he'd been. I wondered why he had returned. He lay beside me that night to keep my bony body warm and we joined for the last time, out of habit more than any other reason. We conceived our third son.

The pregnancy, and Adam, forced me to eat and drink, to take care of my body, and slowly I returned to health. Adam was with me for the birth of this child. A long painful delivery after which I could muster no joy in the babe he placed in my arms.

'A son to replace the one we'd lost,' he said. He was wrong. Having Seth dulled my heartache but didn't heal it. When I held him I felt nothing. No rush of love as I had with Cain, no impatience as with Abel. There was only relief that the birth was over and my body was rid of his. I had no milk and no desire to feed my child. No love left to give. He turned his head away from my breast and cried until Adam took him. He wanted me no more than I did him.

Adam brought a woman from the tribes to wet-nurse and take care of Seth. And himself. I heard them at night, under their furs, and the appreciative sounds that she made to Adam's ministrations. I felt no jealousy, only exhaustion. And relief. She was patient with Seth, attentive to Adam.

She was even kind to me in a distant way, which I appreciated. But she had no interest in my garden beyond raiding it for food, no concept of the family we had been, or from where we had come. I asked her once what her god was like, if he was as harsh as Adam's and mine. She told me she praised the earth with its dark and fertile soil. She gave thanks to the moon which brought the tides and seasons, the winds that cooled, the rain that watered, and the sun that warmed her. She was amused at the thought of a single entity creating all life.

Adam forbade me from speaking about God with her.

'They are not like us, Eve. She is childlike and innocent. Don't burden her with your melancholy.'

They stayed with me until I healed and Seth was strong enough to travel. Then Adam left with his new son and his new woman. There was nothing between us, not even words. I never saw Seth again. I heard he did well with his life and that I had a grandson, Enosh. But Seth never sought me out, and neither did I he.

Without my family, this place held no meaning. I wandered aimlessly about my garden for days before coming to the decision to leave. The last thing I remember seeing was the dried gourd on the altar as I headed east in search of Cain.

8

FRAUD

It is forbidden to kill; therefore all murderers are punished
unless they kill in large numbers and to the sound of
trumpets.
Voltaire, "Rights" 1771

THE SOUL EXODUS FROM HELL THAT SURGED PAST MY bonfire at the beginning of the night dwindles to a trickle. There is only the odd straggler whose steps are slowed by guilt, shame or regret. Some that dawdle have no fixed destination with no happy memories to guide them. Some linger by the gates, afraid of what awaits, reluctant to face their loved ones, preferring the familiarity of their tortures.

The opportunity for a demon to secret itself within the crowd has passed. Now it must outrun me or outfight me. I swing my arms, keep loose and limber and alert for sudden movement. They watch me too, waiting for me to drop my guard. I shift from one foot to the other and adjust my grip on my sword.

'Eve, the great redeemer,' Lucifer calls to me from atop a stack of tires. He affects boredom by flicking an imaginary speck from his spotless shirt. 'Still believe your presence brings propitiation?'

'Just let me do my job.'

'As you wish.'

He waves his hand and demons swarm from the gates over my bonfire. They scream and whoop, careless in their attack. Some are crushed underfoot and succumb to my flames, adding new bodies to my pyre. I've seen this tactic before—they hope to smother my fire early on in the proceedings.

Demon flesh burns with an eerie glow reminiscent of phosphorus, and like the thirteenth element, their bodies spontaneously burst into flame. I wonder if that is why it is called the devil's element. Their skins burn away to reveal desiccated black muscle, yellowing bone, and a red ichor similar in composition to human blood. Demon flesh is a swift conductor of heat and puts on a magnificent display. After the first shock of brilliance, the light dies back and the bodies shimmer with violet waves. Many times hotter than a blue flame, this heat forces me to stand well away from the bonfire for a few moments until the flesh is consumed and turns to ash.

A demon, red and black, mid-sized and badly burned, its wings no more that tattered ribbons, is the first to make it through the flames to my side. It plants its cloven hooves on a teetering log and beats its chest, bellowing for others to follow. Skeletal wings outstretched, it roars and thrusts its scarred face close to mine, and attacks with claws and fangs. I raise my sword and with one stroke hack its head from its neck.

Others come. I cut, left and right. Limbs fly and heads fall. My actions are swift—I do enough to dispatch one and move on to the next. I don't tire easily, but I cannot maintain this pace all night. I choose my adversaries, challenging the least damaged, allowing those still alight to run past, trusting the flames to dispose of them before they reach the junkyard perimeter.

'It would appear you are more like my brother Uriel than I realized,' Lucifer says.

'You're just jealous.'

'Of what?'

'I have a chance to redeem myself.' I stumble over a corpse to stab a ram-faced horror between the eyes and cut the legs out from under a spider-legged beast.

Lucifer leaps from his lofty perch, getting closer to the action. 'You think I want redeeming?'

I should heed the soft change in his tone.

'You want forgiveness as much as I do.'

'You've got that the wrong way around. I have no desire to return to servitude. I like my reign in Hell. I don't need God to tell me what to think or do.'

'If he forgave you, you'd be back faster than I can behead this wretch.'

I grunt and stagger and cut down a demon fluttering by on smoldering wings. A backhanded swipe and its head rolls. Lucifer gives a soft chuckle.

'Just like my demons, you seem to think everyone else has it better instead of making the best of what you have.'

'I am nothing like your demons.'

'No. They would not hesitate to take what I offer. You refuse your heart's desire and there is no one standing in your way.'

'You're in my way. I'm in this mess because of you. Don't compare me to your vile spawn. They have no right to pass onto Earth.'

'Have they not?' His arm lashes out and snatches a

demon from my bonfire. Lucifer blows gently and the flames searing the demon's flesh vanish. Its wounds knit. One demon, slightly singed and a little pink in places, stares, bewildered, at us. Lucifer passes his hand across its face and croons softly. As his fingers move over the ugly features, the features shift and offer a moment of translucency.

I see beyond the mottled skin and razor teeth to what lies beneath. And in that instance, there is more than a transparency of flesh. I see beyond muscle and bone to the spark within, whole and radiant. That trapped incandescent fluttering is familiar. So reminiscent of the discarnate cortège earlier this evening. Within this demon beats a soul; the signature of God the Maker.

At last it becomes clear; that overwhelming despair that emanates from every demon and pierces me, is the pain of a soul incarcerated within this form. This is their real torture, not some fire in Hell. The torment in their eyes comes from within. I cannot believe Lucifer does this with God's blessing. It is no wonder they fight so ferociously for one night of freedom, to taste again the life they lost. Lucifer's boast that he is the creator of his minions, created in his image as man is in God's, is a lie. These are merely his distortions.

'What chicanery is this?'

Lucifer drops the demon. Rejoicing in its healing, it whoops as it races off into the night in search of a child to torment through nightmares, or to play on a woman's insecurities, or drain away a man's courage. His demonstration complete, Lucifer dusts off his hands and looks at me.

'I offer you another glimpse of reality and you accuse me of fakery.' He clicks his tongue against his teeth in reprobation. 'Did you know that arms dealers sell weapons to both sides in a conflict? The true victor of war is commerce.'

'And what need has God of commerce?'

'His currency is devotion.'

I lower my sword and the next demon runs free. 'How did you persuade these poor souls to swap their God dollars for yours?'

'They swallowed His rhetoric, as you do. Followed His instructions to the letter. When they died, he sent them to me! Oh, the irony.'

'So you corrupt the souls of the dead. They're not your creations at all.'

'Now, now, Eve. It's the first law of thermodynamics—energy can be neither created nor destroyed. I give them a makeover. I fashion the clay into something more pleasing. After that, well, call it therapy, I help them work out their issues.'

My enthusiasm to stop the fleeing demons wanes. Several run past me and I make no attempt to catch them. 'God didn't send these souls to you to be used as batteries.'

'Why does He keep sending souls, Eve? If He doesn't like the way I run things, wouldn't He send them elsewhere?' He grins, showing white, even teeth. 'Don't feel sorry for them. They all get what they think they deserve.' He cocks his head as if he has just had an idea. 'Maybe that's your problem too. Do you think your deeds here, tonight, are worthy of Eden?'

I glance at the fire, burning heartily, fueled by blue beech and demon flesh. The ground before it is slick with ichor and blood. Lucifer waves his hand and the bodies of those I felled disappear. Only a few heads and loose limbs remain. A reminder of my exertions, enough to trigger my guilt. It is hard to view my massacre in the same light, but I will not let his words turn my resolve.

One small woman against a demon horde. I face thousands in a single night. I keep people safe in their homes. I stop Hell's corruption from filling the world. A small voice warns, hubris is a sin, and the irony of my circumstance looms large. To return to my home, I must deny the souls trapped within these demon bodies entry to theirs: I am outcast turned gatekeeper.

'Get out of my way!' I yell, tightening my grip on my sword.

It is harder to kill them now I know what lies within. I look away before the end, unable to watch the light extinguished in their eyes. Lucifer cheers, goading them to run faster, fly higher, strike harder. He appears to revel in the spectacle. He needs to dominate, to show me we play by his grace, not God's.

Three die at my blade. Their flesh melted, eyes glaring from charred faces. I release them from their current condition, but return them to their eternal suffering.

Forgive me.

Lucifer boos from above. He pretends to keep a distance, to remain passive, but unlike God, he can't resist interfering.

There is no sign of the demon tide slowing. Instead, the caliber of opponents rises. The brash young fools give way to a wilier contingent. Wild-eyed and idealistic fighters with a hunger for freedom, these demons have self-control and a greater sense of self-preservation. They prefer to get past me without injury, drawing their claws for defense rather than attack. Speed and nimble footwork are their focus.

Lucifer cheers for each one that makes it into the night. His interventions are intent on maximizing my failure. Capricious, he encourages both sides; he wants me to accept his offer and the best way is to defeat me while appearing to support me.

As I defend myself, I keep my gaze averted, for behind each grotesque face I see the imprisoned soul. Perhaps I am doing this all wrong. Is Lucifer right? Am I still here fighting year after year because I believe it is what I deserve?

More demons rush past and I let them go.

'Poor show,' Lucifer calls from his vantage point. A trick of the light gives his black outfit a Tyrian purple hue, befitting Commodus at his games, watching gladiators die for amusement. 'If you have no stomach for the fight, you know what to do. Say yes to my offer.'

'If you keep pressing me, I'll say no now.'

There is a flash of fear in his eyes, for a moment, no more. How absurd for the devil to be afraid of a woman's rejection. Is it because he wants me or because he doesn't want God to have me? He lounges back on his tires and claps his hands.

'On with the show, then.'

I am not willing to fight for his amusement. I lower my sword and there is a cheer from the bonfire as several smoking demons jump from the flames and run to freedom.

A thought strikes me: what if the test God set Adam in Eden was discernment, not obedience? I might have misinterpreted my test as well. Mercy and forgiveness are the sacraments I seek from God, yet I have been merciless in my persecution and destruction of these demons. Assuming them to be Lucifer's fabrications, I set myself above them, dispensing justice and thinking their quest less valid than mine. But now I know they are also God's creatures, my penance becomes ambiguous. I believed my God to be harsh, once. He meted out punishments with swift retribution and his heart was closed to mercy. That God condemned my son and me to loneliness and hardship. From that God, I turned away. The irony is that I have modeled my idea of penance on the old God I rejected, and not the one from whom I sought salvation. I expected mercy from God yet dealt none to my adversary.

Demons stream through my fire and sidestep past me. Some are still wary and others stick out their tongues like cheeky children. The word spreads of my concession and the stream becomes a torrent. I stand back and watch the demons rejoicing as they scurry past me, affectionately patting out flames on each other.

'Lost your nerve?' Lucifer shouts. 'He'll be so disappointed in you.'

No more disappointed than I am in myself.

9

SACRILEGE

> None answ'ring the great ends of humane kind,
> But This one rule of Life; That shews us best
> How God may be appeas'd, and mortals blest...
> John Dryden, *Religio Laici*

AFTER I LOST MY SONS, I SHUNNED GOD.

I lived lifetimes in hedonistic excess, searching for illicit pleasures. I flitted between religions, followed other deities, worshiped false idols. And all the while I searched for Cain, believing reconciliation with my son would bring me solace. Instead, I met another man who brought me peace.

At the time I lived in Aegyptus during the reign of Tiberius Claudius Nero. The efficiency of Rome with the majesty of Egypt. Also, plenty of hot running water, a great invention of the times. I arrived from Greece in the guise of a widow and exempt from the *tributum capitis* tax levied on men in the provinces, I was able to accumulate wealth, quietly and substantially. As a hereditary noblewoman with the right to own land, I had more rights there than in many lifetimes after.

My plantations in the fertile Nile Delta grew the crops the Roman Empire craved. I held no chattel slaves or Shabti —I had no need of handmaidens in the afterlife. Life was ordered and comfortable, and I was content but for news of Cain.

After a few years, I grew restless. Even Alexandria, when compared to Rome or Athens, was little more than a sleepy seaside port that swelled with tourists in spring and autumn and sailors the rest of the year. When I was invited to spend Passover in Jerusalem with friends, I leapt at the chance of civilized conversation and decent wine.

I accompanied my first harvest of the year, winter wheat and flax, to Alexandria and from there, I booked passage on the grain fleet that sailed monthly from the harbor. The trade routes had reopened after the *Mare Clausum* of the winter months when it was too dangerous to sail, and the port seethed with activity.

Excited, I stood on the deck of the heavily ladened vessel under the tightly furled sails and listened to the cries of the gulls overhead, and the shouts of the sailors. The deck below my feet trembled as oars hit the water and by stroke and glide, our journey began on the late afternoon tide as Alexandria grew smaller. The red sun hung low in the sky, resting on the buildings that hugged the shoreline. From its promontory, the lighthouse cast an ominous shadow over the ship. I shivered at the omen, and made a warding sign to the Goddess Tyche, asking for her blessings for the voyage. I found the Greek Fates more accommodating than my previous deity.

Tyche answered my prayers and we sailed an uneventful one hundred and forty leagues to Pelusium, where the fleet split with some ships heading to Rome. For two more days, we traveled the same distance again, hugging the coastline from Raphia, to Gaza and then Ascalon. My wares were unloaded and transferred to oxen-drawn wagons for their week-long trip to Jerusalem. I chose the faster option, at two hundred times the price, and hired a carriage which promised only a day and a half of jostling.

The city that stood proud on the hill had been through many changes: from the small hilltop fortress that David conquered, to the beautiful city of Solomon, and the ruins of Nebuchadnezzar. Now it enjoyed the grand vision of Herod the Great. Approaching the city from the Mount of Olives, I was greeted by the sight of its gleaming golden temple, shining like a second sun above the city. We passed through the Golden Gate and stopped in the temple grounds. I unfurled my protesting limbs from the carriage seat and stood in the shadow of the greatest monument to God in the world. Those familiar feelings of rage bubbled beneath the surface. In need of exercise, I left my bags in the charge of a porter and walked through the Xystus markets in hope of diversion.

There was a frisson of excitement in the air at the coming Passover celebrations. Palm fronds lined the streets, and the crowds filled the markets in the squares to bursting. Every corner was packed with vendors peddling the mundane and the exotic, and the smell of spices roasting and street food made my mouth water. I smiled at children playing with hoops and spinning tops, exchanged strategies with men playing checkers. I lingered at the stalls of the tailors, displaying decorative needles in their tunics, and the dyers with their adornments of colored rags, showing bales of beautiful linens.

Salo and Hermia, my friends, lived to the west in the Upper City of Jerusalem. Their home was a magnificent white marble villa that shone like snow on the desert. Hermia rushed out to greet me.

'Eve, it is so good to see you.' She hugged me close, wrapping me in a cloud of fragrant calamus and hyacinth. 'I swear you look no older than the last time we met. Is there some witchery in the waters of the Nile? The porter delivered your things. Such a big sack of figs, you spoil us!'

'There's frankincense for you too.'

'How kind. We will light some tonight at the feast. You're not the only special guest, you know.' Hermia gave me a sly wink and leaned close to whisper in my ear. 'We are to be honored with the presence of Herod Antipas tonight.'

'Is that wise? I hear he is favored by neither Romans or Judeans at present.'

Hermia linked her arm through mine and led me into the cool interior. 'It amazes me how you hear these things on your farms, Eve. The talk is all about his new wife, Herodias and her daughter Salome, and that beastly affair with the holy man. Who asks for a head? They will be there tonight, you know. What could Salo say when he asked to bring them? Quite the scandal, but I'm not one to gossip. After all he is still the tetrarch, and it is a great honor for Salo to host him at Passover,' she paused to draw breath. 'I have been up since dawn worrying about everything. It has to be perfect. You must wear something exotic.'

'I don't have anything suitable. There's not much call for it on my farms.'

'We will find you something. Don't worry.'

And so, I found myself that evening reclined on a couch in a crimson gown, with my hair in oiled ringlets, and my eyes kohled, eating locusts and olives with figs and bread made from winter wheat. I didn't say anything about Herod and his cruel stepdaughter, but it was obliquely referred to at the tables, discreetly at first, but with increasing abandon after each new flagon of wine. The other popular topic of conversation was about a Nazarene who was preaching dissent to a large following.

'Have you met this renegade, Yeshwa, Lord?' someone asked Herod. 'They say he can perform miracles and calls himself the son of God.'

Herod smiled and raised his cup. 'I would like to see one of his miracles for myself.'

'Maybe he can reattach heads,' someone muttered, and laugher rang out at that table. Herod looked over, expectantly.

'He is here in Jerusalem, preaching of his new god, as usual. Perhaps you might witness a miracle, if the authorities don't arrest him first.'

'He's angered every priest and dignitary in Jerusalem. No regard for authority.'

'But he's so popular in Galilee and Judea.'

The more they spoke of this mysterious man, his sermons, his followers, the stories of his miraculous healing of the incurable poor, the more I began to wonder. Could he be Cain?

The conversation drifted to different matters and I lost interest. Seated near to Herod, I watched him laugh and joke with his companions, and I noticed his eyes drift to Salome more often than they did to Herodias. Then the lamb was brought to the tables with the obligatory oohs and aahs, and the Passover ritual was completed. Replete, I went to my bed and resolved to see this Yeshwa while I was in Jerusalem.

I awoke to a commotion outside my bedroom window. My room was dark. I stumbled to the window on unsteady legs, and opened the shutters to a grey pre-dawn sky. In the yard below, I saw shadowy figures, dressed in the garb of priests and temple guards. There was an air of menace about the way they stood. A man, his hands bound and his head bowed, was flanked by two guards with spears.

My sleepiness was displaced by curiosity. It was odd that such visitors would come here at this time. I willed him to look up so I might see his face, but he did not. Salo came into the courtyard and spoke softly with the priests. Their conversation was too low for me to catch but Salo shook his head and glanced often at the prisoner. The priests were insistent. After more discussion, Salo threw his hands into the air and stalked back inside the house.

I kept watching, and soon Salo returned with Herod who wore a red cloak and despite the early hour, seemed cheerful. The guards gave him a parchment which he read swiftly and tossed to the ground. He ordered a chair to be brought for him and sat in the yard in front of the prisoner.

'It would appear the mighty Pontius Pilate is in need of my assistance.' Herod addressed the man in his booming voice. 'I am invited to interrogate a dangerous prisoner.' He paused for effect, leaning forward to address the shackled man. 'One who would have my title.'

My heart skipped a beat as I craned forward, again hoping for a glimpse of the man's face. Could it be the Fates had brought him to me—the man they'd spoken of last night at dinner? The one who preached against the proscribed religions. An itinerant man whose charisma drew crowds. The man who sought to be king. Could he be Cain?

At that moment, the sun rose above the clouds and the man lifted his face to its warmth. I was disappointed and relieved. It wasn't my son who stood before Herod. I should have known. This man didn't have Cain's mark—that air of violence, warning of danger. This man was ordinary. For, while not awed to be in the presence of Herod, neither was he arrogant in his stance. It was hard to equate this barefoot humble man with the evangelist who incited an uprising of thousands.

'Come closer,' Herod said, his tone cordial, almost reverent. 'Pilate has sent you to me so I may assess your worthiness. Your guilt or otherwise is in my hands. Do not displease me. I have heard of your miracles, healing the sick, feeding the poor, preaching of a merciful god. Prove to me your prowess and I will see you released.'

I recognized the longing in Herod's voice for answers; it mirrored my own.

The man turned his gaze to Herod and when he spoke, his voice was clear and unafraid.

'You may not release me. It is not my Father's will.'

I gasped at his audacity and saw the angry rigidness of Herod's body. He stood and stepped close to Yeshwa and I strained to catch his harsh whisper.

'It is not my wish to see you dead. Pilate is no friend of mine. Give me the chance to deny him his quarry.'

Yeshwa nodded. 'I thank you, but that decision is not yours to make.'

Herod's head snapped up with surprise. 'Your father wishes you to suffer?'

'I willingly do my Father's work. My reward will be to walk at His side in His garden this very night.'

My heart skipped a beat. His words seemed directed at me. I rushed out of my room and to the front door of the villa.

'Eve, you are not dressed! Come away.' Salo caught my arm, but I fought him for a place in the doorway. This man who called himself the Son of God spoke of returning to a garden. God's garden. Perhaps it was the garden I once knew. If he could return, then so could I.

But this man described his God as benevolent, declaring Him forgiving. I could not reconcile that with my own experience. My God showed no compassion towards me or my son. The God I knew was capricious and judged people on a whim. I'd heard the stories the Jews told of Him. He drowned thousands of innocents, sent pestilence and famine across Egypt. Brought down His wrath on those that displeased Him just as He'd condemned me to hardships unimaginable. That was the God I recognized. Yet, this man saw Him differently. Was it that possible? I had so many questions I wanted to ask this Yeshwa.

'I can set you free to walk in any garden you choose,' Herod said. 'There will be no walking with your father if Pilate has his way. He will have you killed like a common criminal.'

'Which he is, my Lord,' a priest said. 'This man has forbidden the payment of taxes due to the emperor.'

'That's not my concern,' Herod snapped. 'As long as he pays mine.' He turned back to Yeshwa. 'A small miracle to satisfy my curiosity. Is that too much to ask?'

'You have a duty to Tiberius,' the priest persisted.

Herod swung around to face the priest. 'You wish me to favor Romans over Jews? Is his rule more to you than mine?'

The priest impressed me with his fortitude. He held his ground and looked Herod in the eye. 'We have no king but the emperor,' he said.

Herod turned away, his face red with fury. 'Do you have nothing to say?' he bellowed at Yeshwa.

I willed Yeshwa to defend himself, to prove them wrong, but he did not.

'Fraud. Abydocomist!' The priest mocked. 'Where is your god now?'

Yeshwa neither argued nor submitted as abuse washed over him. His eyes caught mine. He knew me, knew my struggle. I had to speak with him.

'This man is not worthy of my attention. Take him to Pilate.' Herod stood and walked away.

I grabbed Salo's hand. 'Bid them break bread first. Show hospitality and kindness that it may reflect well on you this Passover.'

Salo nodded and stepped forward to speak with the priests. I rushed to the kitchen to fetch yesterday's bread and water for the prisoner.

I walked towards him with a racing heart and shaking hands. He looked into me, his eyes finding my soul. His hands were warm and gentle as he took the bread from my fingers. He smiled and it lit up his face, wiped away the lines that furrowed his brow. He broke the bread and gave half to me. We sat on the hard ground of the yard. He took my hand in his and bowed his head.

'Pray with me,' he said, offering me comfort when it was he who faced certain death. Unlike Herod, I didn't doubt his spiritual ability. He had the same aura as the angels I'd met before—Uriel, Michael, Lucifer. I sensed the power of his charm, although he did not unleash it on me. I'd lived too long and seen too much to be skeptical of a miracle or two. I was curious about his God and how He differed from mine.

'But He hears me not,' I said, the words choking me.

'Pray louder. And more often.'

I laughed, and the bitterness poured out. 'To whom—the God who cast me out without a second thought? The God who took my sons and caused my suffering?'

'To the God who loves you.'

'I don't know which one that is. I've prayed to An, Enlil, Enki. To Marduk and Inanna. To Atum, to El and Asherah, to Brahma and Shangti. I've even offered sacrifice at the altar of Zeus. None of them answered me.'

'There is only one God. Our God, Eve.'

He knew my name. I panicked and started to rise, but he caught my hand.

'I am His son, and I tell you, He loves us all. Tonight I shall stand by His side in Eden.'

His words brought tears to my eyes. 'Tell Him I'm sorry. I wish I could go home too.'

'Tell Him yourself.'

'He ignores me.'

'It is you who ignores Him, you who has wandered far, Eve.'

Yeshwa took my cold hands in his burning hot ones. At first, I thought him feverish with illness, but the heat spread along my arms, through my body, filling the dark empty hollows of my spirit with a primal fire. That heat burned away the years of resentment, hatred, and loneliness that festered within. It refreshed me with hope and a strength of will I'd thought impossible.

'Show me how to find my way back,' I begged.

'My time has run out,' he said as the guards approached. 'Come to me three days hence and you will see the truth for yourself.'

They took him to Pilate who conceded to the priests and they crucified him that very day. At midafternoon, the sky turned black and Jerusalem stood dark and silent for moments as he died. I wept, believing my chance at redemption died with him.

On Sunday, I woke before the sun. Yeshwa's words echoed in my head—*come to me*. I dressed and left the house before Hermia and Salo rose, and walked to Golgotha, the place where he had been crucified. Nearby stood a garden and I was drawn to it. I walked along the paths, admiring the beauty of the spring morning, when I came upon a tomb hewn from rock with a large stone beside the entrance. On the stone sat Yeshwa, basking in the morning light.

'Welcome, Eve,' he said.

'You are alive,' I said stupidly. My mouth was dry and the words were no more than a croak. I stumbled towards him and could not stop myself from reaching out and touching him, to confirm my eyes saw true. His flesh was as warm as mine, his eyes clear and gentle and I was overwhelmed by the comfort that poured from him.

'You are immortal like me,' I said.

'My immortality is God-given, my life is a blessing, before and after. I am not caught like an insect in amber,' he said. He held out his hands to show me his wounds unhealed. I felt unclean beside him. Tainted. Stunted.

'Help me, please. Tell me what to do.'

'Pray,' he said. 'The answer will come. Your transgressions can be undone.'

I kissed his feet and would have lingered, but I heard the sound of women's voices approaching. My heart was filled with joy for the first time in so long. I knew now I could be forgiven and could go back to Eden. Like Yeshwa. I just had to prove my worthiness.

I raced back to the city, to the temple on its lofty perch and stepped into its darkness. Alone, I prayed to a more sympathetic god, begging for a way to cleanse my debt and to return home.

Light, white and gold, flooded my body. Every cell of my being vibrated with the resonance of love. His presence blossomed deep within me and for the first time He spoke to me, through me. Not through Adam. I chose how to hear Him in my heart, to hear His benevolence. I opened my soul to Him until I could bear no more.

Yeshwa was right. My eyes filled with tears as my old doubts tried to creep back. Life had used me up, and I was no longer the girl who walked in His garden. That girl was innocent, but I had done many things of which I was not proud. I tried to speak, but no words came. The floor before me grew wet. For a long time, I did nothing but sob.

'Bless me, Father. I have sinned. Let me prove my worth. Give me a new test of faith.' I spoke the words aloud, to give them more power and to show I had nothing to hide, that I cared not who heard.

'I can resist temptation. I will not succumb to Lucifer's honeyed words again. Allow me to make repair for my sin. Please bring me home to be as I was.'

I did not grasp the enormity of my request. His response was to fill me with more light and love until I glowed more brightly than Uriel's sword. Caught up in His ecstasy, I thought I understood the task He set me. As I had brought Original Sin into the world, so must I banish it. To conquer my demons, I had to conquer Man's demons. I was so greedy for absolution, I agreed without a second thought. Anything to end the empty ache inside. I walked away from the temple with a lightness to my step.

IN OCTOBER OF THAT YEAR, I walked into the desert and stood before Lucifer and his demons. It was the first time I'd seen him since our afternoon in Eden. My mouth was dry and my hands shook, and I told myself it was the fight ahead that unnerved me.

'Delicious Eve. What brings you here?' Lucifer greeted me. We both knew my purpose.

Woefully unprepared, I suffered a terrible defeat that night. It would be an exaggeration to say I stopped more than a handful of demons from their revelry. Broken and bruised I dragged myself away at dawn. But I returned the next year with horse and cart, and built my first bonfire.

Each year, I achieved a little more. Each year, I understood the enormity of my task, my debt to humanity that had to be repaid.

But tonight, I doubt my assumptions. I began with good intentions of righting wrongs, but what if I misunderstood the Nazarene? Do unto others, he said, and so I did as was done to me. That made me part of the process. I got caught in a cycle. The Nazarene was a single voice against the crowd. I thought I was doing the same, standing against demons year after year, but I was wrong. I perpetuated this farce. To be part of the change, I cannot simply walk away, I must end the show.

10

SIMONY

> One must always do what the Devil forbids.
> Martin Luther, Wittenberg Hall, 1530

'Turn back!' I shout at the escaping demons but I don't strike. I have lost this battle between conscience and compassion, knowing what lies within their hideous forms. Emboldened, one demon lashes out at me. Its tail whips through the air a hairbreadth from my face. I bare my teeth and it scurries away.

Lucifer smirks down from his throne, high above the proceedings. His vantage point offers him the ability to control his minions and watch me. A nod of his head and another wave of demons rushes the fire. Lucifer waves his hand and an infernal wind catapults them through the flames unscathed. On my side, they reorientate and scamper away. I keep my sword lowered by my side. He laughs and sends more.

He wants me to fight. He wants me to fail. He wants me to accept his offer.

I let those that run have their night of freedom. Those that attack me feel my steel.

A bold upstart comes at me, all claws and fangs. I am rewarded by a sickening crunch as I cut through a neck of bony sinew. Its head topples to the ground and rolls across my feet coming to rest with eyes wide with surprise staring up at me. This demon is juvenile; smooth hide, small wings, and underdeveloped claws. I guess it is newly hatched, or whelped, perhaps only days old. The taste of bile fills my mouth, and I turn away, unable to look at its features. There is no honor in killing babies.

My fury builds at Lucifer's for sending them out. He suffers no compunction in dispatching the helpless to our battle. He sees me glaring and he shrugs, affects a bored expression.

'Come on,' he says. 'It's your last night. If they don't fight now, when can they?'

Dropping from his perch, he joins his generals on the other side of the fire.

He changes into a gleaming silver tracksuit and sneakers, a flashy beacon among the black and red. No spot of soot or ash tarnishes his purity. He wants me to notice his radiant divinity as he consorts with his generals. He points and snaps his fingers, and although I am too far away for me to hear his words, I see the disbelief on his generals' faces as they stare across the battlefield at me.

Then come the howls and groans and headshaking. Their visceral protests. Word spreads through the ranks and I watch its progress in the physical reactions of the foot soldiers. That ripple through the ranks; the jerk of heads when they first hear the news, the slump of shoulders in disappointment and then the stiffening of spines as dismay shifts to anger. He's told them this will be their last fight. A genius move to ensure the best battle possible.

I look back at Lucifer. He is huddled in conference with his generals. There's an intensity to their war talk. They're plotting something big.

It scares me that Lucifer is getting involved in the strategy rather than remaining neutral. It also bothers me that this scheming is happening so early in the night. It was a mistake to confide in Lucifer.

Something hits me from behind and I stumble. A claw gouges my back. Its owner gets past my blade and locks its gnarly talons about my neck. I gag on the fetid breath as it brings fanged jaws down to snap at my head. Twisting away, I bring my arm up to block, but a stony foot slams my wrist to the ground. I hear bone snap and my fingers lose their grip on my sword. My attacker drops his weight onto my chest, its legs astride my body. Knees crush my upper arms as claws squeeze my throat. My legs flail, trying to find leverage. I try to call out for help. To whom? There's no one here for me. My eyes look skyward. No sound escapes my constricted throat. My vision blurs. I cannot breathe.

There's a sharp snap, and the weight from my chest lifts. My would-be executioner falls to the ground. His lifeless eyes stare up at me. Lucifer kicks him aside. He crouches beside me and with a smirk, he wipes a smudge from my cheek.

'Is your God even watching?'

I can't answer. I hear myself coughing. My throat is painful as I struggle to take in air, but already I am healing; the bones in my hand knit and the skin on my back feels tight.

'Are you ready to stop?' He offers me his hand.

I ignore it and stand up. I turn my back on Lucifer and look at the demons on the other side of the fire.

'Don't thank me,' he says before he disappears back to his generals.

He wants me to fail—to have no choice but to accept his offer but Lucifer's plotting encourages me to put my own plan into play. I have a scheme, long contemplated, but never used. If this is my last fight, tonight is the only chance I have to test my secret weapon. I wipe my shaking hands on my jeans. This strategy depends upon the element of surprise. Attack hard, attack first.

With the tip of my sword, I draw a circle in the surrounding dirt.

I am not a magical being. I have no talent in that area. My longevity is my only benefaction, and it is, in essence, a lack of God's gift. But my time on Earth has been well spent. I have read and learned from many and their tutelage has opened my eyes to one basic tenet: if you don't have the skill yourself, use someone who does.

My original plan was to capture a demon within a binding circle to power the thaumaturgy of my pyre. The prospect of success was always slim—demons resist capture more than death.

But now I have a better idea. One that will change everything if it works.

He is waiting for my answer to his offer. He will come if I call. Deceiving the Great Deceiver is a daunting task, but... I stand at the center of my dirt circle and try to look subdued.

'Lucifer, can we talk?' The nervous crack of my voice is genuine.

'About?'

'You know.'

He comes without hesitation. There's a light strut to his step as he walks through the flames towards me. He scans my face, searching for clues. I keep my eyes fixed on him, drawing his attention so he doesn't notice the circle. He grins, wearing confidence like a cape.

I smile as he steps into my circle, unsuspecting. Toe to toe, one eyebrow raised, a lazy smile plays about his lips. My heart beats hard, expecting to be caught out. I lick my dry lips.

'Say it,' he whispers. 'Pledge to me.'

I nod. My breath shudders through my lungs. I step back, taking care not to smudge the line, and speak a single word.

Lucifer frowns. He recognizes the holy word of binding known to the few. Uncertain if he heard me correctly, he tries to step towards me. It takes a moment for him to understand what I have done.

Every log, branch, stick and twig, each piece of kindling and twist of paper integral to my pyre is inscribed with a ward or rune, curse or spell, charm, or imprecation. Hedgewitchery binds them to the Earth and fortifies them against demonic power. Ancestral *magick* calls on feminine power from all civilizations from all times. Over the years, I scoured grimoires and pagan tomes, harvesting the knowledge of dark mistresses. Every evening for years, I carved and traced each component of my bonfire with symbols and characters, concealing enchantments in the natural curve of wood. Small and large, my fire calls on every known feminine conjury. Many times, I tried to invoke those hexes only to discover I have no talent in that arena. Other years, the spells perished with the wood, but tonight Lucifer is my conduit. He is the yang my yin *magick* needs.

His mouth tightens and there is venom in his eyes.

'End this forever,' I say. 'Forbid your demons from leaving hell. Give me your word and I will stand down and set you free.'

'And if I do not?'

'Then I will do what I must.' Trembling, I look away.

His generals know something is wrong. I hear a howl, and I feel Lucifer's mind reach out to them. Demons scream across my bonfire, traversing the burning brands in droves. Wave after wave surge forward to save their leader.

'I need an answer now.'

'Never.'

I choose a tall, tusked fellow. It shrieks as it steadies itself, revealing claws and tongue. As it crouches ready to spring, I speak a curse under my breath. It requires no force on my part to carry the curse to the target; Lucifer's will is already directed there. The log beneath the demon explodes, flaring white hot, an imploding star. A wave of impact expands around it, incinerating surrounding demons in the fallout. The blast rocks me on my heels.

Chaos erupts. Screaming, pushing, biting mania, as others try to avoid the same fate. They scatter in all directions, including skyward. Those falling crush those below.

Lucifer howls with fury, but my circle binds him tight and he must comply with my commands. His generals pace their territories, no longer concerned with keeping order.

'You will pay for this!' he snarls.

There is a shimmer about him, as he tries to marshal his strength but it is mine to control. He cannot so much as change his clothes without my permission. My secret weapon comes to the fore: All the *magick* that over the centuries women have been persecuted for wielding.

Divine feminine power.

11

VIOLENCE

> The fatal flaw of magic lies not in its general assumption of a sequence of events determined by law, but in its total misconception of the nature of the particular laws which govern that sequence.
> James George Frazer, *The Golden Bough*

THE SYMBOLS CARVED INTO THE WOOD SPRING TO LIFE, lucent amidst the gasping flames as I speak my cantrips. I have trapped the strongest force of evil within my circle and my hands shake as I close fingers about imagined tendrils and draw from him a surge of power. Sorcery courses through my veins, cold and slow, a chemotherapy that chills, injecting me with supernatural sight. Hues I've never seen before wash over the junkyard. A purplish brown, sickly yet mesmerizing, lights the sky. Black clouds lined with fluorescent green swell and contract overhead.

Lucifer glares at me. The blackest cord stretches from his chest to mine. Every thought of his mingles with mine. I shiver, giddy within a swirling miasma. His voice echoes inside my head, cajoling one moment, petulant the next, and a fury hotter than lava rises in my gorge. I inhale the smell of smoke and diesel, tires and dust, and will the supernatural to withdraw.

Grounded in my reality, I grow stronger. I smile at him, surprised at my audacity. I chant louder, more confident in my words, and set about bursting the demons who step onto my cursed logs and succumb to my sorcery. A macabre fireworks display begins—the twisting shrapnel of their bodies as they swell and explode. Flaming chunks of flesh and fountains of gore spray everything, including me.

Slow applause reverberates.

Lucifer stands untouched within my circle, his clothes pristine. Eyes flash, his mouth twists, his shoulders quiver.

'You outdo yourself, Eve, turning this *maleficium* against me in His name. Bravo! What chance have my minions against such unexpected ordnance?'

I keep chanting and gesturing. The incantations are tricky and in languages I haven't spoken in a long time: Sumerian, Elymian, Sanskrit, Tamil. The ancient tongues have more power than modern ones. My tongue twists an earthy power that plumes deep into the soil, far below the scars left by man's destruction of land and sea, to a primordial font. Tapping into this energy revitalizes me, but only for a moment. That euphoria is diluted with the acidic bile that Lucifer brings to the equation. He scowls at me and taints the energy, but he can do no more.

The timbers are layered in an exact pattern, forming a compass rose of bewitchery. Thousands of spells and hexes waiting in sequence for execution. I ignite the top layer in sections, using my spells with care, and targeting demons to avoid wasting hexes. When the top layer is spent, I dig deeper to the enchantments below. These curses are not enough to last until dawn, and at some point, I will have to stop demons the old-fashioned way again, but for now I have a powerful alternative.

The generals keep their eyes on Lucifer. I wonder if he can communicate with them without my knowledge. I doubt it. I am privy to his feelings and his focus is on me. All his anger pours in my direction. And his fear that he underestimates me.

The older demons comprehend what I have done; the younger ones grow quiet, sensing something amiss. The stream of demons entering my fire slows. This second wave is smarter and tries to cross in the wake of the fallen, hoping that way will be clear of spells. I dig deeper and draw up the spells buried below. As the wards rise to the surface, more Satan-spawn are burned and maimed, but the horde is not deterred. As they climb over the broken bodies of their fallen comrades, bone cracks under hoof.

'If you send them, I will smite them,' I shout at the generals.

'They won't listen.' Lucifer says. His shoulders are slumped, but his eyes burn.

'Order them to stop!'

'You're the one giving the commands.'

The look he gives condemns me.

'You forced me to take this action.'

'You delude yourself, Eve. You've sunk this low all by yourself.'

I lash out at the oncoming demons with renewed vigor. The look in Lucifer's eyes haunts me but I move back and forth, ensuring there is no rhythm to this dance, no expected move, as I lash out with word and sword, spell and strike. One large demon leaps over an exploding log and swoops at me. I stumble as I swat him aside.

His generals watch my strategy, their eyes follow the

patterns of my wards, searching for weakness. I pause in my recitations and choose a different sequence. Lucifer stands within his circle, scowling as his demons explode. He casts me murderous looks and mutters to himself. I try to focus on what he's saying, but it causes me to stumble with the ancient words and my spell fails. He notices.

Lucifer projects his thoughts into my head—before they swirled, now they suffocate, filling every crevice of my mind. Hundreds of voices, all his, talking at once in both my ears. I cannot think to recall the words I learned. My spells fail, the logs fizz like sparklers wasting away; the enchantment weakens, too transient to hold. Lucifer crows and intensifies his efforts. His demons seize the opportunity to swarm the bonfire. I can't waste my precious advantage. I close my eyes. Focus. Block out his presence.

It is a dangerous move. With my eyes closed, I have to rely on my other senses to tell me where the demons are. I listen for the crack of a trodden branch, the whiff of meaty sweat. I direct my attacks by intuition. Their screams, the pop and crack of hoof on twig, the heat of explosions, and the thud of flesh. Hot blood splashes against my skin. Lucifer screams with frustration and the voices cease their chatter and retreat in moody silence. I open my eyes.

He is not watching me anymore; his attention is on the demon horde. They have stopped their advance. I recognize a huge demon, one I have seen many times behind the gates; Focalor, a powerful Great Duke of Hell with thirty legions at its command. It appears as a man with eagle wings and comes to the fore, drawing others around in a huddle to dispense orders. Under the chaotic chatter of voices, Lucifer conveys instruction in tongues before I can stop him. I marvel at his ingenuity as I curse him.

Focalor picks up a smaller demon and throws him high

onto the pyre. With a head start, the demon whoops and flies over the burning brands towards me. I invoke a curse and it bursts into flames. Focalor repeats his maneuver with another demon, throwing him in the same direction. The other generals follow suit, hurling their victims at the same spot, over and over again, until it is void of charms. They are clearing a path.

Lucifer watches my lips. I hear him muttering under his breath, weaving a spell of his own, one I cannot control. He ought not to be able to do that, but he is Lucifer Morningstar and my knowledge of his abilities is lacking. My lips feel swollen, bee stung. I lisp over my words and the spells fail. The demons advance and leap from the pyre onto me. My sword sweeps upward and severs an ear, cuts through a torso, and splits a head in two. But I cannot defend myself and curse at the same time. I step aside and let them run past me. They succeed in clearing a way through my wards.

Lucifer laughs, and it fuels a peculiar rage within me. I lash out with berserk fury, cutting and slashing without restraint at any unfortunate demon running too close. My hexes abandoned, I cut a swathe through the runners, but I cannot maintain this intensity and they know it. The generals watch me, intelligence in their eyes as they time the passage of their forces through the flames. They send bigger, wilier foes; dark knights that strike with savagery, giving no quarter. Cruel and vicious, bigger than gorillas, these warriors are well-trained and skillful. I have no choice but to resort to my final *coup de main*.

'I call upon the powerful flame, Nesert.'

Lucifer moans as the force of the final word leaves my lips and every stick and brand of wood flares with sickly light. An eerie hush spreads over the junkyard; the wash of a nuclear detonation. The silence before the final movement of my sonata.

My voice carries over the desert as I speak the words from *The Book of the Dead* to raise the Lady of Terror:

> *'Hathor, set aside your poisoned flacon,*
> *   assume the mantle of Sekhet anon.*
> *Lady of Death unto the fray, dispense justice,*
> *   and evil allay.*
> *Lady of Pestilence, Eye of Re, Queen who*
> *   eats demons, feed on their ire.*
> *I offer sacrifice!*
> *Oh, Red Queen. Gulp down their hearts, eat*
> *   your fill.*
> *Bring forth the blood lust as they burn*
> *   according to your will.'*

The desert exhales. Its breath, the stale wash of old death, overpowers the smell of fresh blood and sweet burning flesh. Decay, centuries old, rises from every crevice. Pestilence more virulent than any Ebola of Hell rolls in. The desert inhales, a rasping slither of snake. Locusts' legs chafe and the whine of a million mosquitos anticipates her arrival. The desert exhales light, bright as the midday sun. She Who Is Powerful is come.

A demon hurtles from the flames with a wail. Its flesh erupts with sores and pustules, eyes burst with pressure, and limbs tear from its body with a wet suck. Logs catapult in all directions, spinning in search of targets, exploding on contact with unerring accuracy. My fire swells beyond the expanse of the paranormal pyre, transformed by angry air, and the spirit I summoned from her ancient slumbers. Nothing else exists within my vision.

'She will pay, my beautiful boys. Stop it!' Lucifer is shouting. Cursing me. His voice cuts through the agonized cacophony.

I close my eyes and cover my ears. But I cannot block the smell of rotting flesh. The iron meatiness that pervades. I fall to my knees, begging forgiveness for unleashing this devastation.

'Enough!' I plead for her to stop but the Mistress Lady of the Tomb has no intention of abating her slaughter.

Demonflesh crumbles to dust as the rage of Sekhmet whirls about me, uncontrollable after millennia of confinement. I hear sobbing and am unsure if it is me or Lucifer, or us both. I cower, protecting my face from the sandstorm that whips and tears at flesh of all kinds. That high-pitched, unnatural squeal deafens me to all other sound and presses me in obeisance to the ground. The Eye of Re's bloodlust scours the junkyard.

Minutes or hours pass as I cower in submission, but at length, the stench lessens and the wind falls away. Oily smoke descends and there is only the sound of the crackle of my fire.

I am unhurt, but through the smoke, I see the bodies. Thousands upon thousands of them, mangled and destroyed. They shroud my pyre and the ground before it. All of the junkyard and the desert beyond as far as I can see is littered with bodies, whole and dismembered, limbs jutting at impossible angles. Now and again a body bursts, releasing a cloud of powdery funerary dust that sticks to my blood-slicked skin.

Beyond the bonfire, the way to Hell is clear. Hushed and shaking, the lucky stragglers hide behind the gates. None dares venture forth. I see them eyeing their fallen comrades. The pain and fear emanating from their trapped souls hangs heavy in the air.

I could not imagine the extent of the annihilation I unleashed. So much death and destruction, so many dead. I pray the thirst of Nesert, the Red Lady, is quenched.

Staggering to my feet, I see Lucifer crouched on the ground in the circle, weeping softly. I lurch towards him. My foot scuffs the edge of the restraining circle, severing the continuous line. Before I can repair the damage, Lucifer vanishes and takes with him the body of every dead demon.

12

WRATH

> Where then shall Hope and Fear their objects find?
> Must dull Suspense corrupt the stagnant mind?
> Must helpless man, in ignorance sedate,
> Roll darkling down the torrent of his fate?
> Samuel Johnson, 'The Vanity of Human Wishes.'

My bonfire is ordinary without its hidden enchantments. The necromancy from the desert recedes like the tide, leaving its debris behind; the broken washing machines and tires strewn haphazardly about the junkyard. Even Hell's overwash is diminished. I stand amidst the garbage and take stock of the devastation.

On the far side of the fire, the survivors realize Lucifer is free. They stop cowering, straighten and regroup. There is confusion among them. Normally there is a strict hierarchy to the Armies of Hell that no one breaks. I don't know if it is a reward program or the threat of severe punishment that keeps order among the ranks. The foot-soldiers search for someone capable of giving them orders. They search for the generals but they are either dead or have fled. They wait for Lucifer's command. None comes. Lucifer is gone from this place, and all is in disarray.

A huddle forms and I hear grunts and screeches. A young demon is sent off, running back to Hell. They wait. So do I.

I feel empty with Lucifer's ensorcellment sucked from me. Wrung dry. Every cell in my body screams from abandonment. An addict crashing from a high, I shiver and hug my arms about me, willing the agony to pass. The deeper pain from my conscience won't fade so easily. Using him as I did, I broke our unspoken pact. He was never my combatant. Until tonight. Like any addict I justify my behavior—he broke the rules first. He left me no choice but to play my trump card. My body starts to heal and the pain of withdrawal is replaced by grief.

I hear the beat of a drum. Deep and primordial. A summoning that enters my bones. I glimpse formless shadows moving beyond the gates. A foul stench rises from the ground. I gag. I wipe sweat and ash from my face and grip my sword with trembling hands. The remaining demons cackle manically and stomp their feet. They know what's coming.

Dark shadows higher than a house loom forwards. Eight bloodshot eyes gleam from the blackness. The shadows coagulate into four beasts.

Denizens of the deep. Lumbering behemoths, frankenbeasts cobbled together from animal parts. I get a good look at the first one; a lion's head with an eagle's beak sits on a bear's torso. Scraping on the ground behind is a scorpion's tail. The others are different permutations of the same recipe. I have not faced these monsters before.

The ground shudders with each step they take. The stacked appliances teeter precariously. A dryer tumbles to the ground. The beasts' mouths gape wide enough to see their tongues of glowing coal. Acidic drool spills from their lips, sizzling into the earth. I can sense no tormented soul within, only a rage at being dragged to the surface, at having to face me. I suppress the urge to run. My knuckles turn white as I raise my sword to meet them.

They move slowly but with purpose. One stops and swings its head, a tusked goaty visage, left and right. It howls and slumps and turns away from me. Behind, small demons with whips and chains rush out and try to turn it back. The creature howls as the metal hooks on the end of the whips bite into its hide. One handler darts around to the other side and wraps a chain around its leg. The creature howls again, and with one swipe of its paw sends the handler with the chain flying. It tramples the others underfoot as it runs home.

The other beasts don't acknowledge its departure. They continue towards me. One fewer gargantuan gives me little comfort, but still my knees threaten to give way.

Their handlers shout and lash at them, forcing them to cross what remains of my fire. Fiery eyes squint as they focus on me. The ground undulates as they trample over the logs. The sweet nutty aroma rises as their hooves sink into the crumbling remains of logs and bones, crushing everything to dust. Puffs of ash rise into the air.

I wait for the giants to step from the flames, and in their moment of unbalance, as they lurch from branch to solid ground, I strike. A massive limb, too thick to sever with a single stroke, swings at my head. I duck and stab upwards, tumble to safety.

Cold eyes reflect the image of my blade. No flicker of fear or mercy survives in those bottomless pits. Bile fills my throat.

'I don't want to harm you!' I shout.

One of the beasts charges: a giant with the face of a crocodile and the pincers of a crab. I feint to the left to dodge its snapping jaws, and slip in a bloody slick. Its tail smacks me across my shoulder. The spiked edges, sharp like fishhooks, tear at the skin between my greave and breastplate. Its pincer-like grip closes over my shoulder and pulls me towards its jaws. Fetid breath assaults me, razor teeth waiting in anticipation. I heave my sword upward, through the roof of its open mouth into its brain. Death doesn't loosen its grip on my shoulder. I pull away and the claw comes with me, still buried in my flesh.

The lion-headed beast roars and lava spews from his beak. He ignores his demon handlers and turns back to follow his companion.

I hear words in my ear, whispered from a distance but clear as a bell. 'If you could die, I'd let you.'

'I don't need your help,' I shout.

Shaking with anger, I pull the claw from my shoulder, spinning around ready for the next adversary.

Disembodied laughter surrounds me, eerie and bitter. 'Do you believe you have survived all this time by your merit alone? Only by my grace, Eve, mine alone. What you did today was not very smart. Alienating your only ally.'

I think of the countless occasions over the centuries where he has come to my aid. When he called respite to give me time to recover, and in those worst times, when he used his power to heal my wounds. I like to think God works through Lucifer. But it is possible he intervened for other reasons. For his reasons— entertainment or punishment or spite.

'You're only an ally when it suits you.'

'Harsh and ungrateful. No wonder God and Adam abandoned you.'

My scream of frustration is real. 'So quick, like a spoiled little boy, to cry foul if I don't play by your rules. Show yourself!'

'You are treacherous, like all your kind, Eve.'

'It is only the weapons in our arsenal that differ, not the tactics.'

'I'm impressed by your deceit and lies.'

I feel the heat in my cheeks. 'I had a good teacher.'

Lucifer's laugh fills the air. 'Apart from my charming company, what keeps you coming back every year?'

I freeze. It is odd that he asks me this, now. My unfinished business is the same as it has always been. Only one thing has stopped me from ending this charade of a penance. A hope deep inside me that is slowly dying. The mother who no longer waits for her child to come home. It kept me locked in indecision for so long.

To my left, something rustles. The demon handler comes at me with his whip. I turn too late and am slow to raise my sword. The demon is thrown into the air, pushed away by an invisible force.

'Stop helping,' I yell.

Lucifer laughs. 'God's champion needs no help. Shall I leave it to Him to save you?'

An eerie howl fills the battlefield and coldness pierces me. The change is sudden and complete. Lucifer is gone, not just from my vicinity but from Earth. He retreated to his domain and his minions. Unharnessed from his yoke, they are free to act at will.

The sound of buzzing grows louder. Tiny, winged demons gush from the blackened gates. Like locusts, they swirl through the air in formation and as one they plunge earthward to join their remaining hooved brethren. They fly at me, pecking at my eyes, pulling my hair.

I scream as I shield my face with my arms, twisting left and right trying to protect my eyes. I catch one in my hands, but its wings are like knives that slice my palms.

Wave upon wave of demonic mosquitoes bring a cloud of demented terror. I am overrun by a dirge of their soulless emotions, and their weightiness, physical and emotional, forces me to my knees.

The giant beast crashes towards me, impervious to the biting cloud that surrounds us.

I fall to the ground and lie there in the slippery demon ichor and my blood, sooty with ash and bone dust. Hunched over, my head tucked low, I pray for the onslaught to pass. I hope they'll tire of me and leave to seek their pleasures on Earth.

I am this way when I hear the squeaking. The pound of thousands of tiny feet coming at me. A sea of demon rats sweeps through the gates beelining for me, their burning ember eyes fixed on their target, their shrieks ear-piercing.

I hate rats.

They swarm over me, their feet pound my skin, toes gripping my clothes as they climb up and over. Thousands of them, jumping onto my back, piling one on top of another, pressing me down. Smothering me with their furry bodies. I gasp for air, thrashing as I struggle to free myself of the vermin.

The smell of rancid fur fills my nostrils. I gag and scream as the biting begins, savage and everywhere, but they poke their heads into my mouth, biting my tongue. I bite back and spit out the head of a rat. My saliva tastes of its blood but I dare not open my mouth to spit again. They are in my ears, my nostrils, biting my neck, my scalp. I can't move, can't scream. Too many and more keep coming.

I gasp for breath between clenched teeth. Is it my ignominious fate? I can't heal if there is nothing left of me.

13

PESTILENCE

> When I am dead, open my grave and see
> The cloud of smoke that rises round thy feet;
> In my dead heart the fire still burns for thee...
> Hafiz of Shiraz, 5

IN 1347, I LIVED IN RAGUSA WITH MY LOVER OF TEN years, Blazh Sorko. With Blazh, I found a gentle happiness I hadn't expected. I intended to stay with him for as long as possible. But news came to Ragusa that winter that changed everything.

I'd heard rumors over the years of a man who rode with ÖzBek, the Great Khan of the Tartar-Mongol Golden Horde. A man so lucky in battle he bore no scars despite his reckless ferocity. This man claimed knowledge of ancient battles and advised the Great Khan on strategy. He rode with ÖzBek for forty years until the Great Khan's death, and now rode with the new Khan, ÖzBek's son, JaniBek. It was rumored that this man didn't age. I assumed the man was Adam until a new rumor concerning ÖzBek's conversion to Islam came to my attention.

When ÖzBek took the faith, he demanded everyone else in the horde to convert as well. This man refused. His fate should have been death for disobedience, but no man had been able to administer his punishment. It was whispered that the man was cursed to immortal life by a god he despised. The Golden Horde lay in siege outside the walls of the Genoese city of Kaffa and I was certain that the man who advised JaniBek was Cain.

When I told Blazh I intended to visit a besieged city, he shook his head and sighed.

'Is it your wish to be ravished by barbarians, my love?'

'I'll be perfectly safe,' I assured him with a confidence I didn't possess.

'But why do you want to go there? Barbarians and Genoese.'

The emphasis of his disdain lay with the latter. He caught my arm and pulled me into his lap. 'With spring coming, I thought we could spend some time together on the islands—swimming naked in the sea, making love under the stars...' His lips began a slow trail of kisses down my neck.

'So tempting, but I have urgent business in Kaffa.'

Blazh gave me a knowing look. 'Is this a different business than usual?'

'What do you mean?' I asked.

'Don't treat me like a fool, Eve. I've known you long enough to recognize that haunted look in your eyes. I don't question or object to your travels each autumn. I welcome you back with open arms. But I've held you through the nightmares. Whatever you do on those trips affects me too.'

I tried to stand but he held me fast, his hands gripping my hips.

'You know I love you. I accept that you hold secrets

from me, when I have none from you.' There was pain in his voice and a lump formed in my throat.

'You wouldn't understand,' I said, looking down at his hands.

'I understand you are not like other women, Eve. You do not beg me to marry you. You accept I cannot because of my family name. You are as sweet and playful as the day we met. My brothers are jealous and my friends think me a lucky man. I will not press you for details, I am content with what you give me. Whatever the cause of your pain please know there is nothing that could make me love you less.'

I wrapped my arms about his neck and rested my cheek against his.

'Thank you. This is a matter from long before we met.'

'Let me come with you. It's not safe for a woman to travel alone.'

'You are needed here.' I didn't want him to come. I was not ready to share Cain with anyone. 'The families will not allow you to travel to Kaffa. What if you were taken hostage?'

'What if you are taken from me? I could not bear that,' he said.

I thought of all the people who were taken from me. The people I'd had to move on from to keep my identity secret. I was weary of the deception. I looked into Blazh's eyes and saw the love and trust. I nodded.

'I will return, and I will tell you every secret about me when I do.'

*

I SAILED from Ragusa to Venice and on to Kaffa on a merchant vessel flying the banner of St. Mark, announcing proudly to the world that it enjoyed the protection of La Serenissima, the Republic of Venice. The journey was uneventful and uncomfortable and my expectations were low, so when I sailed into view of the harbor, I was astounded at the enormity of the Genoese fortress rising before us. The walled fort sat on the curve of the bay, pale limestone glistening in the sunlight. A large rectangle of walls and towers stretched from the water's edge up a steep incline to a vantage point that overlooked the bay. Formidable—as was needed in such a dangerous location on the edge of civilization. Beyond the fort, lay Lysaya, the bald mountain, rich in gems and gold and supposedly the gathering place of witches. The primal savagery of the land reminded me of my early years out of Eden. I shivered and drew my cloak closer about my shoulders.

Twelve towers, square and crenelated, guarded the city and one of them was built over the water so it looked as if the structure floated on the turquoise mirror of the Black Sea. Our vessel changed its colors to the red cross on white of the Genoese Republic as it drew near. We approached from the east and docked at the sea-gate in the floating tower. I entered the stronghold and saw the wonder that was Kaffa.

Linking the towers were limestone walls as high as six men standing on each other's shoulders, and thicker than my outstretched arms could span. They were the reason this fort had resisted the assault of the Golden Horde for nearly three years and provided a serenity that belied the violence outside. The ground sloped steeply upward from the sea towards a gleaming citadel built of marble and limestone. There was an inner wall about the citadel where my guide found me rooms, simple but clean with meals included. I left my belongings and walked around the city, along paved avenues, through courtyards with lavish fountains and scented gardens, past churches with marble countenances and stained-glass windows. The relaxed bustle of the streets surprised me. I'd imagined it deserted with the ongoing siege, but trade was brisk in the bank, and stalls displayed silks, furs, and jewels. Guards stood chatting with merchants, worshippers visited churches, and there was laughter and ease in daily life as if nothing sinister lay outside the city walls.

I spied a *hammam* near my lodgings and headed there excitedly to have the rigors of my sea voyage soaked and massaged away. I stepped into the moist chambers of the women's section where I found several pools; one cold, one hot and one tepid for relaxing. I sat on a stool as the masseuse lathered and rinsed me. It was glorious to lie back and have my back scrubbed with ground almonds and honey and my hair washed with rose water. My limbs grew heavy and limp as she rubbed the knots from my stiff muscles. Afterwards, I sat in the steaming waters of the hot pool, up to my neck in liquid happiness, and closed my eyes.

'Is it your first time here?'

I opened my eyes to see an older woman in the water beside me. She wore intricate gold earrings and a heavy chain with a jeweled crucifix about her neck.

'Forgive me, but I haven't seen you here before. I come every day. My name is Alagia.'

'I am Eve. I arrived in Kaffa today.'

'Wonderful. So lovely to see a new face. Life gets dull here and I long for news of Genoa.'

'I'm sorry I cannot help you. I came from Ragusa, via Venice.'

'Ah.'

The dismissive tone and dimming of interest in her eyes

at the mention of the backwater Ragusa and of Venice, the sworn enemy of her beloved Genoa, gave me hope our conversation had run its course.

'What business is your husband in that brings you here?' she asked. Alagia's eyes fixed on the ring I wore on a chain about my neck: Blazh's signet ring with the Sorko family crest.

'I am here alone,' I said.

'Ah.' This time there was curiosity.

'Well, you have chosen an interesting time. And a fortunate one of late. Kaffa is rejoicing now that God has come to our aid.'

'What do you mean?'

Alagia kissed the cross hanging about her neck. 'God sent a pestilence to strike down our enemies. The heathens are falling like flies. Thousands die each day, brought down by our prayers. This siege will soon be over, the Lord be praised.'

'Indeed.' I nodded and swam to the steps to climb out of the pool. I had been praying and fighting demons on Samhain for over a thousand years and God had answered none of my prayers. I wondered what they were doing right that I wasn't. Alagia followed me.

'My husband is confident his next shipment will come by land. The merchants of Kaffa have been held to ransom by those pirates controlling the waterways.'

'They have you at a disadvantage,' I agreed.

Alagia sighed. 'It is the way of commerce, as my husband says. Supply and demand. So, what brings you to Kaffa if not a husband?'

I stepped out of the water and pulled on my robe. I wondered how much to tell her. Either the massage or the soothing bath had lowered my defenses.

'I believe my son is with the horde,' I said.

Alagia crossed herself several times. 'I shall pray for you, my dear. They have taken too many of our young men hostage. I can help you get word to him if you wish?'

I was shocked at her casual offer of assistance and it must have shown on my face. She smiled and patted my hand.

'I send my women out to the camp regularly. A woman with a basket of washing or food can get almost anywhere. It's how I know what is going on outside the walls. Most make it back without too much trouble. We can get word to your son.'

'I would be in your debt.'

Alagia clapped her hands and an attendant appeared.

'Paper and ink,' Alagia demanded. The girl bowed and scurried off to comply. We sat in an alcove in a small courtyard, with glasses of mint tea and I stared at the blank paper for long moments, my mind blank as I searched for words to say to my son. After so long none were adequate to express my longing to see his face. I toyed with the quill for a long time before I set it to the paper and scratched a sentence, woefully lacking.

> *I am here. I long to see you.*
> *Please meet me.*
> *Eve.*

I folded the note and wrote *Cain* on the outside and passed it to Alagia.

'I will send it with my girl tonight,' she said as she tucked the precious paper into her sleeve.

'Please thank her for me. I will pray for her safety,' I said.

Alagia laughed and sipped her tea.

'Slaves don't require thanks or prayers, my dear,' she said. 'She does as she is told. Don't trouble yourself, the men are rough but the girls usually survive. If this one doesn't make it, I will send another. Your son will get your message.'

The tea in my mouth tasted bitter. I put down my glass and wiped my lips.

'I'm sorry, I must go,' I said. 'Thank you for the company and for your help.'

'Drop by again. I should have word of your son in a few days,' she said.

I dressed hurriedly and left the *hammam* at odds with my conscience. I had known Kaffa was famous for its slaves, and its slave markets were the busiest in the region. I abhorred the practice and would not have come otherwise. I abandoned my principles for Cain.

I climbed to the fortress ramparts, those sections where citizens were allowed to walk safely, and looked down into the valley between us and the mountain. Sprawled for as far as I could see were the thousands of men and their tents and horses that kept us pinned in this place. I saw the orange flicker of fires burning in the distance, sending clouds of black smoke to linger above. When the wind changed direction, it brought a waft of acrid foulness. They were burning their dead. Alagia was right, disease was rife in the Mongol camp and the only thing protecting us from it was the wall on which I was standing.

Shielding my eyes, I scanned the horizon, hoping for a glimpse of Cain. I knew it foolish; it was impossible to detect a single person among the thousands, but it wasn't reason that made me linger and long. I had traveled this far against all logic and I would risk anything to be with him. I prayed for the swift return of Alagia's slave.

The insistent ringing of bells woke me in the early hours of morning. I pulled on my clothes and headed into the streets with the rest of the city's inhabitants. Dark shapes arced across the lightening sky accompanied by a strange whirring. I heard screams coming from a few streets north and wet thudding sounds. Thinking I could help, I headed towards the commotion but stopped at the terrible sight that greeted me.

Chunks of rotting flesh, smeared pus, blood, and other foul liquids coated the cobble-stone street and the walls. People ran in all directions, covered in blood and muck. I pushed closer, against the flow of those fleeing. The chunks of flesh wore remnants of clothing, undershirts and bits of leather, the skin was mottled, the muscle ravaged by disease and crawling with maggots. The stench made me retch. I recognized the signs of this pestilence. I'd read treatises on its contagion and remedies for its treatment. A plague to rival that of Egypt, feared by all. The Black Death.

The strange whirring sound began again, and a young man pulled me into a nearby doorway just in time to avoid being hit by flying bodies of Mongol warriors. The bodies burst on impact, splattering everything with fetid juices. The horde had found a use for their dead—catapulting them into Kaffa.

For hours the bodies rained down. They piled high in the streets, attracting rats, repelling people. By evening, the skies overhead filled with slow-circling vultures. The city guard loaded body parts onto wagons and wheeled them down to the harbor where they were tipped into the ocean to drift out with the tide. But the bodies came faster than we could clear them away. Thousands of bodies, on streets, in barrows, bobbing in the sea.

Within a day, people began to sicken. Coughing and fevers were the first signs. I went to one of the churches, where people were bringing their sick, to help as best I could. They laid the ailing on the floor. I washed the black boils with vinegar, burned lavender to draw out the evil humors, and brewed chamomile teas to calm stomach bile. The smell of vomit and sweat and feces was overpowering. After days of caring for the dying I walked out of the church into the gardens beyond. I could hear wailing and chanting for the dead all over the city.

'Eve, come sit here, share my meal,' Alagia said. She sat on a stool under a tree, dressed in silk brocade, her dress high-waisted, her skirts billowing, in the latest Genuese fashion. Her hair was held back by a jeweled headdress with a Moorish design. If I hadn't been so hungry or tired, I might have refused her invitation, but the golden pastries and the cup of wine she held out to me crumbled my resolve.

'Thank you,' I said as I took a pastry and bit into it. My mouth filled with fruit redolent with cinnamon and sugar. 'Hmm, delicious.'

'You are most remarkable, Eve. I certainly couldn't deal with the sick as you do.'

I took a big swig of wine to stop myself from replying.

'Is there anything to be done for them? Is it not better to isolate the afflicted to stop the spread of the contagion?'

'There are many treatments, Alagia. Bathing with rose-water and musk mallow is advised. And once the lesions appear, olive oil can be rubbed into the skin.'

'But do they work? Tell me honestly.'

I finished the pastry and sipped some wine. 'Most of the

afflicted die within three days.' I didn't elaborate on the agony that accompanied their dying. 'Willow bark and valerian keeps them comfortable until then.'

Alagia sniffed. 'The barber-surgeon, Argono, is offering a curative for eight *genovino*. Eight! I could buy a dozen horses for that. What do you know of it?'

'I've met him. He comes to lance boils. I don't know the efficacy of his potions, but I can tell you that so far nothing works. I've found treatises by Galen and Avicenna in Arabic in the library. When I have time, I'll translate them to Latin for the physicians. Perhaps we will find the answers there.'

'Take care not to anger God, Eve. It is better to take the poor souls to a priest than follow the advice of heathen doctors.' Alagia raised her eyes to the sky and crossed herself. I almost laughed.

'Excuse me, I would like to walk a little. Thank you for the meal.' I rose and dusted the crumbs from my apron. 'Have you heard from my son?' I tried to ask casually although my heart was racing.

'My maids say he is not with the prisoners. There is a man called Cain who is kept close to the leader, JaniBek.' Alagia leant forward and pressed my hand, her expression contrite. 'I am sorry to tell you, my dear, there are rumors that they are unnaturally close.'

Now I did laugh, out loud and heartily for the first time in days. 'Please let me know as soon as he replies.'

The streets I walked down resembled my earlier expectations. The only traffic was the over-ladened wagons hauling the dead to the seashore. The only sounds the wails of the mourning, the moans of the dying, the cries of the carrion eaters, and the scurry of vermin. And the church bells. They rang out every hour, reminding everyone that the Black Death was God's punishment for the sinfulness of humankind, and the only cure was prayer.

I stayed at the treatment rooms, sleeping on a makeshift cot when I could no longer stay awake. We had to turn people away. With more dead than living in the city, there was no one to bake bread, no one to clear the streets.

One morning, I woke with a cough. The ache reached into my bones and fever racked my body. I wandered out into the street, searching for the Argono to take over my duties for the day. A coughing fit robbed me of any strength, and I collapsed against a pile of dead bodies. Through my delirium, I thought I heard Alagia's voice. I dreamed hands lifted me from the putrid streets and carried me to a soft bed. I thought someone tended to me. I imagined they carried me to a ship and sent me away from Kaffa.

I WOKE FROM THE FEVER, weak but free of disease, and I learned I had not dreamed my rescue. I had been on a ship bound for Constantinople for the last six days. The woman tending me gave me two letters. The first was from Alagia:

> *Dearest Eve,*
> *I pray for your swift recovery.*
> *The last ships sail from Kaffa tonight and I took the liberty of securing you passage. The slave accompanying you is Pačia, a good if dull-witted girl. She is yours.*
> *I am returning to Genoa to my family, my husband has succumbed to the fever. May we meet again under better circumstances.*

God's blessings upon you.
Your friend,
Alagia
p.s. I enclose a note passed to my maid. I
*   hope it is good news.*

The second was a dirty scrap, the writing almost obscured by a large stain. But I recognized the hand and it made my heart hurt to read it.

He had written in Aramaic: *Come if you wish.*

I sobbed and beat the walls until my fists were bloody. In Constantinople, I tried to buy passage back to Kaffa, but word of the plague had spread and there were no ships willing to sail towards death. With a broken heart I continued to Venice, hoping to secure passage back to Kaffa, and Cain.

14

MALIGNITY

> For tho' from out our bourne of Time and Place
> The flood may bear me far,
> I hope to see my Pilot face to face
> When I have crost the bar.
> Alfred Lord Tennyson, 'Crossing the Bar'

THE JOURNEY TO VENICE WAS ONE OF PESTILENCE AND horror. Passengers and crew alike succumbed to the illness. Most of them died. Pačia caught the fever within days of my recovery. I put her in my bed and lay on the floor beside her, listening to her labored breathing. I bathed the foul sweat from her body and fed her willow bark, but when the buboes burst under her armpits, oozing pus and blood, I knew there was nothing more I could do for her. I mourned that she would never know life as a free person in Ragusa. The next morning, the sailors tossed her body along with the other dead into the churning waters as we prayed for their souls.

We arrived in Venice on the tide, with only a handful of people still alive. It was early spring and the city sparkled in the distance. Word had spread of the contagion at Kaffa and that we brought the evil spirits with us. We were refused entry into Venice proper or leave to sail.

The ship docked at the island of St. Mary of Nazareth and they carried the sick into the Nazaretum. I'd never seen such a place solely dedicated to healing and isolation.

I stepped from the gangplank and a young man in a strange beak-like mask approached me.

'Signora, do you have the fever?'

'No, sir, I am quite recovered.'

He made the sign of the cross, and a note on parchment. 'I am sorry, but you will still need to remain here for *quaranta giorni*.'

Forty days. My hopes of returning to Kaffa to see Cain were dwindling. I nodded. 'Of course. I would like to help. I tended to the sick in Kaffa.'

He looked at me as if I were mad but agreed.

He took me inside the Nazaretum where there were more men in beak masks. I learned later the beaks held herbs to purify the air as they breathed. Inside the rooms where the sick lay, the air was dry and acrid, thick with smoke from aromatic herbs burning in thuribles that covered the stench of the dying.

The man led me through to a small room at the back with four beds.

'This will be your room, signora.'

I looked around at the bare floor and walls and thought of my cozy home with Blazh. I wondered if the Mongol horde was still at Kaffa or if they'd moved on now the city's inhabitants were dead or fled. I thought about the next forty days; the smell of vomit and feces, and the eye-watering smoke that wafted through from the main room.

My days followed a precise routine. Before the sun rose,

monks attended to care for the sick. They came and chanted prayers all day. They complained that the air was too 'stiff' with evil. Doves were brought to the island and flown around the rooms to break up the air. The monks rang bells to frighten off evil spirits, but I think they frightened the birds more.

There was less medicine here than at Kaffa. The richest patients bought powdered "unicorn horn" for more than Argono charged for his concoction, and with less effect. They died the same as the poor, in agony and within three days. I wrote to Blazh from Venice describing the horrors and telling him of my temporary confinement. He wrote back telling me the illness had reached Ragusa and begged me to keep safe and to return as soon as I was able. There was news from Kaffa too: the conflict between JaniBek and the Genoese had been resolved and the horde had moved on.

I spent less time in the Nazaretum. The only chores available to me were cleaning the messes. Herbs were only used for burning to ease the vapors, not for easing pain. That was the province of the Church. I finished my translation of the treatise of Galen into Latin and put it in my sea-chest, ready to take back to Ragusa.

Walking around the island provided me with some distraction during my countdown to freedom. It took no more than an hour to do a full circuit as Venice proper called to me from across the waters. I watched the little boats that rowed out each day bringing provisions, and correspondences, and doves.

At the other end of the island was the burial grounds. The three grave diggers who visited the island each day by boat from a neighboring island came at sunrise and left after midday. After a few days of nodding at me from a distance,

Giam, Marsilio and Cecco invited me to join them for lunch.

'Come. Sit, signora,' Giam said with a wink and a smile.

'Where do you come from?' Cecco asked as he offered me wine and olives. Their accents were different from those I'd heard in the Nazaretum.

'Ragusa. And you?'

'We are from the south. There is no one brave enough to do this job in Venice.' They laughed and toasted themselves with wine.

'Why are you here? You are not sick and you are not a priest or a doctor,' Marsilio said.

'I sailed to Kaffa on the Black Sea looking for my son. I was sick with the fevers but I am well again.'

'A beautiful woman like you, traveling alone?' Cecco shook his head as he poured me more wine.

I laughed. It felt good to talk and flirt a little with these men who shared my interest in travel and politics and were better company than the pious inhabitants of the island. They brought out more food; layered meat and dough and cheese cut into squares that they called *lasana*. Delicious. After that, I visited them every day and brought a contribution to share.

'Eve, did you hear?' Giam asked, 'the scholars of Venice have declared us to be in a time of "pestilential atmosphere." A planetary conjunction has caused the rise of this epidemic.'

'Blasphemy!' Marsilio said, and they all laughed.

'Better to listen to the flagellants than to the scholars,' Cecco said. 'They are rising again, showing their love of God by beating themselves senseless.'

'Better to rely on our own wits. Salute!' Giam said.

On my last day, I went down to see them for the last

time. They were arguing with the monks about opening up the old graves to add more bodies. I lingered back, unwilling to expose our friendship to the scrutiny of the judgmental monks. After much gesticulating and heated words, the gravediggers sat down and opened their lunches. The monks left in frustration and my friends beckoned me.

'What do they think, we can make more space on such an island as this?' Giam flicked his fingers in frustration at the sea.

'What will you do?' I asked.

'What can we do? Layer them like *lasana*, and pray for forgiveness,' Marsilio said, kissing the gold cross he wore around his neck.

'We have a gift for you, Signora Eva,' Cecco said. He handed me a small glass bottle. 'This is the *stregheria* that keeps us safe. Thieves' vinegar. Excellent for grave diggers, and robbers.' He gave me a smile to show a newly acquired gold tooth. I opened the stopper and sniffed the liquid. I smelled cloves and rosemary, bitter wormwood and sage, well steeped in vinegar.

'Thank you.' I hugged them tightly and blinked away tears. I would not be sad. I was heading home to Blazh.

※

Ragusa had not escaped the ravages of this God-sent pestilence. There were no porters at the docks to carry my bags. No Blazh to meet me. I assumed he had not received my latest letter and left my chest at the docks to hurry home and surprise him.

The limestone-paved *Stadun* and the web of streets that led from it were strangely deserted. My home was locked and shuttered, like other houses in the area. I wandered down other streets, all equally empty, with the bells of St. Luke ringing in the distance.

Inside the church, I saw people for the first time. They were huddled on their knees, praying. I recognized my friends, Milosh and Elena, and made my way over to where they sat. They welcomed me with hugs and smiles.

'We prayed for your safe return, Eve,' Milosh said.

'The streets are deserted. Where is everyone?' I asked.

'There are curfews. Those who haven't died are in the churches. The noble families have sequestered themselves away from the sick to avoid the contagion.'

I sighed with relief. 'Thank the saints Blazh is safe with his family.'

Milosh shook his head. 'He would not go. He waited for you to return.'

'Where is he? I have so much to tell him.'

Elena burst into tears. 'Oh, Eve.'

A numbness crept over me.

'We tried everything,' Milosh said. 'Praying, fasting, even giving him ground-up bone of the blessed St. Ivan.'

'Father Stejpan says it was because he angered God, by...' Elena's voice drifted away but I knew what she wouldn't say.

It was because of me. Sinners were the most vulnerable. Blazh had dishonored his family by refusing to take a noble wife and chosen instead to live in sin with me. And the Church decreed women responsible for carrying the pestilence through their association with Original Sin. My sin. Poor Blazh was doomed from the start.

Numbness turned to pain. I clutched my chest, unable to breathe.

'Sit down,' Milosh said. I knew it worried him that the priests would notice us. It was best to not draw attention.

'I want to see him,' I said.

'He is buried in lime, two weeks past,' Milosh said.

I stared at the statue of Christ, smiling benevolently down on us. What had he said to me on that Sunday morning so long ago—open your heart to God? My heart was broken into a thousand pieces and I had nothing to show for it. In my attempt to find Cain, I had angered God and lost Blazh.

※

I ALMOST DID NOT RETURN to fight that Samhain. The Black Death raged across Europe and all strangers were looked upon with suspicion. I traveled with a group of penitent flagellants as they made their way from town to town extolling the virtue of self-abuse as protection from disease.

Their fervor made me think about my devotion. All those years of turning up to fight for His cause. It had not prevented me from getting ill, not stopped Blazh from dying. Lucifer's meddling and my punishment of immortality saved me. What was the point of all this suffering? The only one who derived any benefit from it was Lucifer. I began to wonder whether what I was doing was the best route to redemption. But I knew no other way, so I made my way back to the desert.

15

ENVY

> It sucked me first, and now sucks thee,
> And in this flea our two bloods mingled be...
> John Donne, 'The Flea'

I OPEN MY EYES TO SEE HIS GOLD-FLECKED IRISES staring at me. There is a quiver of relief in those amber lakes. He kneels beside me, his hand on my arm, his life force infusing me with delicious strength. That familiar shiver of excitement runs through my limbs. He takes his hand away and I sigh, bereft at the loss.

I am on the ground where I fell. I look up at the sky. It's dark, but there is a smell of morning about the chilly air. I cast a glance to the side and see my bonfire. It is little more than a campfire bearing the signs of hours of neglect. There are no demons about us, no beasts, no insects or vermin. The desert is eerily quiet.

I pull my body upright but sitting makes me light-headed. Lucifer rocks back on his haunches and examines me. I flex my fingers and toes, move my head from side to side, stretch my shoulders, check for bites. Everything works. Lucifer tuts and shakes his head. I wonder why he helped me when he is still angry with me.

'You should be more careful. Those wily beggars strike from nowhere.'

'And where are they now?'

'Infesting some city.' He grins, and the sky seems a little brighter. 'Are you going to laze there all night?'

I scramble to my feet. My clothes are bloodied and shredded, but my flesh beneath is unblemished. Thanks to him. I add more wood to the bonfire, blowing on the flames to help them catch.

'Why would you help me after what I did?'

'Why would I not?' He watches me tend the fire.

I tie the tattered edges of my shirt together. 'Does this mean you forgive me?'

'Not in the slightest.' But there is a tenderness in his voice.

'Then why help me?'

He parts his lips to reply and stops. His tongue is just visible between his white teeth. I sense him searching for the right words.

'Thank you anyway,' I say.

'My, my, Eve. Where's the admonishment? After all, you would have healed eventually.'

'Well, if there was anything left. Otherwise,' I shudder, 'He's allowing me to finish my vigil and I wonder at His motive.'

'Give me your answer. It's time to embrace your greatness, Eve. Become the woman you fear. The one I adore.' He whispers, 'Be my queen.'

'Oh, Lucifer.' Perhaps I am lightheaded from blood loss. My body longs for his touch—an after-effect of the healing. I wrap my arms about his waist and press my face against his chest. Standing in his arms, the sweet smell of him intoxicates me. I hear his chuckle against my hair. The heat from his palms sears the skin of my back. This close to him I cannot think straight. His energy flows through my veins, invigorates me. Pure cocaine. I raise my face to him. My lips part ready for his kiss.

'Say the words, Eve.'

My mouth is so dry I can't move my tongue to form words.

'Say yes.' His lips are within reach.

My mouth is open but no sound comes out. I am about to nod when a vision of Cain's face floats across my vision, drawing me back from the abyss. I sigh and stiffen within Lucifer's embrace.

'So be it. *Bellum romanum*,' he says. His hands loosen and drop away as he pushes himself out of my reach. My veins throb, my muscles spasm, and my heart constricts. Withdrawal.

※

BEHIND US, a murmur rises. Across the fire, demons have returned. These are puny specimens, babies and yearlings, blinking with their first view of the other world. The host parts, pulling back like the Red Sea from Moses' staff. From their center, a figure moves towards the bonfire.

Flames lap at her stiletto heels, almost caressing her. Firelight casts a soft filter over her lithe body and highlights her high cheekbones and wide eyes. She advances with an easy grace not once stumbling over logs or bodies. Every sway of hip and heel is a stab in my heart.

I suffer that light embrace of enemies as she hovers her rouged cheek beside my sooty one. She engulfs me in a cloud of vanilla and ylang-ylang. When she pulls back, she is still spotless, none of the blood and grime that bespatters me dares to stain her.

'Eve. How long has it been?'

Not long enough. She leans back, surveying me as she tucks a stray lock of hair behind my ear. Her nails rasp softly down my neck. Admiring her handiwork, her dewy lips part to show pearly white teeth and she winks at Lucifer.

'Lilith.' Her name scratches my throat on its way out. The last time I saw her, she had Adam's arm about her waist.

Lucifer watches us with a predatory grin. Payback.

Lilith toes the head of the young demon handler that attacked me earlier.

'Poor Abdiel, so young and so much potential.'

'What's it to you?' I wondered if she'd made up the name.

'He was my son.'

'You have plenty more.' She brings out the worst of me. If it had been any other mother, I might have consoled her and experienced remorse. I could do neither with Lilith.

Lilith snuggles up to Lucifer and places her head on his shoulder. Her long black hair contrasts against his fair locks; night to his day. She whispers something in his ear, her words too quiet for me to hear. Lucifer nods, and with a wave of his hand Abdiel's head and body disappear.

Lilith lowers her eyes. 'Thank you, darling, it was distressing to see him lying there, butchered.'

Her insincere coquetry irritates me. I doubt Lilith has any more to do with her litters than delivering them. She must have seen thousands of them die. My callousness disturbs me, but she has the knack of revealing my worst traits. She must hate me too: I'd have no mercy towards someone who killed my children.

Lilith kisses Lucifer hard and long on the lips, pressing her breast against his, and arching her back. I can see their tongues intertwined as she moans. Lucifer places his hands on her buttocks and slow grinds her hips to his. There is a practiced air to their actions; it is not solely for my benefit. I should look away, but I am glued to every detail.

He is the one to break their contact. She sighs, licks her lips, and casts a sly glance my way. My fingers itch for a cigarette.

'Is the show over? I have a battle to finish,' I say.

'What's the hurry? Weren't you losing?' Lilith inspects her nails.

'Not against Abdiel.'

She sniffs back imaginary tears and Lucifer gives her shoulders a little squeeze. Their casual affection doesn't escape me.

'That was unkind,' he says.

His rebuke stirs further pettiness in me. Lilith pushes to the fore. The euphoria of being angelically healed fades fast.

'Is there some point to her visit?' I ask.

Lilith gives a throaty purr, low and drawn out. 'It's date night, isn't it, lover?'

Lucifer grins and licks his lips. Licks her lips.

The demons fidget on the other side of the fire, but neither Lucifer nor Lilith seems to care.

'Is there a point to all this?' I say.

'I wanted to catch the last show. It is the last one, isn't it?' Lilith says.

I glance at Lucifer who refuses to catch my eye.

'It is,' I say.

'Hmm. Be careful, Eve. They say all people lie, women to please men, men to please themselves.' Lilith kicks at my fire and ash and embers fly in all directions. 'Oh, and Adam sends his regards.' She faces me, all pretense at civility gone.

'I doubt that,' I shrug, but it is a shock to hear his name from her lips, the lips Lucifer was just licking. Adam always runs back to Lilith.

Across the fire, demons growl and pace. I notice a general standing at the front; Focalor. He escaped Nesert's rampage. He waits for Lucifer's command.

'He said you'd be prickly,' Lilith said.

'That I believe.'

Lilith leans in. 'It was so easy to take him from you. You don't know how to control a man, Eve.'

My cheeks burn worse than if she had slapped me. I see her hand on Lucifer's arm, caressing him. Somehow that hurts me too. There's no doubt she understands the devil better than I do.

'Thanks for the advice.' I turn away.

Her hand grips my shoulder, her fingers like claws. 'If you can't control Adam, how do you expect to control God?'

'I didn't realize I had to.' How much has Lucifer told her about my pact?

'That's why you are still fighting this pointless battle. Why you will always fail. He is the master of this game. I've been where you are. I kept my end of the bargain. He reneged on me. You wait. You'll see. God always finds a loophole.'

'What bargain did you have with God?' I find it hard to believe God would have made any arrangement with her. Lilith smiles. She knows she has me.

'He gave me His word.' She strokes Lucifer's cheek. '"Remove your temptations from mortal men," He said, "and I will remove their slander." Has He done that? My *arse*, He has.'

'And what a lovely *arse* it is,' Lucifer says as he slaps it.

Even in bargaining with God, Lilith has beaten me.

'So you couldn't control him either,' I say.

She gives me a doe-eyed stare.

'What did He promise you, Eve?'

I glance at Lucifer, and he raises an eyebrow, daring me to tell her. It pleases me, in a perverse way, that he hasn't told her already. That he keeps Eden a secret between us two.

She waits for me to answer, her dark eyes filled with inquisitiveness and I am happy to disappoint her. Whatever she learns will find its way to Adam's ears and I don't want him to get wind of my plan. I want to return to Eden alone. Not in Adam's shadow.

'None of your business.'

'Suit yourself.' Her lips purse and her eyes narrow. She turns to Lucifer. 'You promised this would be fun, big boy, but she isn't fun at all. What do you both see in her? I don't know how Adam put up with her for so long. Let's go somewhere more interesting.'

'Please do,' I say.

'The second half of the evening's entertainment is about to start. Go grab a seat. I'll join you later,' Lucifer says with a peck on her cheek.

Lilith makes a move. 'You've been spending too much time with her. If you become boring, I'll have to find a new playmate.' Lilith glances around and rests her gaze on Focalor, standing by the gates.

'He looks fun.' She pats Lucifer's cheek, flips back her long hair and with a swivel of her hips, steps into the fire. Lucifer watches her strut away. She doesn't look back and his face takes on a frown. I could be dancing naked in those flames and he wouldn't look at me that way. Lilith is right; I don't know how to control any of them.

'Why would you invite her?' I ask.

Lucifer runs a hand through his hair. 'To be honest, I hadn't planned to. But you raised the stakes.'

'You're saying it's my fault?'

'That is the problem with playing with fire, Eve. It's so easy for it to get out of control.'

Lilith's tinkling laugh carries across the junkyard.

Lucifer tears his eyes away from her and takes a step towards me.

'No need to be jealous, Eve. I brought her to persuade, not taunt you. I thought she'd help you see the truth. Once you commit to me, I'll banish her from Hell.'

Of course it's all a game to him. Lilith is no less a plaything than I am. He would discard me as easily if someone better came along. Only a fool would believe there was any merit to his offer. Only a fool would fall for those amber eyes and the desire writ plain on his face. There are moments when I feel he is genuine, but those scraps of moments are not enough.

My fury is not for him, or her, it is the rage that eats at me from inside. I think I've made so much progress over the years but one encounter with Lilith and I am almost back to square one.

It is easy for him to pretend. Lucifer's brilliance is not his lies but his selective use of truth. He does care for me. Lilith and God might have had a bargain. But beyond the facts, there is always something he doesn't tell me. He pits me against Lilith and he's the only one who benefits.

APOCRYPHA

> So from the ground she fearless doth arise
> And walketh forth without suspect of crime.
> They, all as glad as birds of joyous prime,
> Thence lead her forth, about her dancing round...
> Edmund Spenser, *The Faery Queen*

I LOOK ACROSS AT LILITH FLIRTING WITH FOCALOR. SHE smiles and waves.

'I don't know why you dislike each other so much,' Lucifer says, fanning the flames.

'Yes, you do.' I whisper the words.

His chuckle irritates every nerve in my body. He grabs my wrist and pulls me in close, chest to chest, breath to breath.

'I think your anger is misplaced.'

Lilith reveals my weaknesses. I blame her in that strange way women blame each other rather than the man. I blame her for my marriage ending, even though my relationship with Adam had turned sour long before she drifted back to him. I blame her for the doubt I have about Lucifer's offer. I blame her for my mistakes. But I won't admit that to Lucifer.

'She ended my marriage.'

'So that had nothing to do with you and Adam?'

'How could I compete? She has everything I lack. Freedom, confidence, independence.' —You.

'You could have those too.'

His lips are so close we breathe each other's air. The image of him kissing Lilith flashes before me and I lean back, twisting out of his grasp.

'No, I can't.' Lilith chose to leave Adam. She refused to obey him, refused to be subservient to him. She had the courage I lacked. God made me for Adam without Lilith's 'faults.' I am the second wife in all ways. The wrongs in Lilith were left out of me and I envy her wholeness. She lives life doing only what suits her. In my mien, selfishness is a dirty word. Lilith thrives through independence. The delicious irony is that the quality Adam is most drawn to is independence. The worse Lilith treats him, the more he wants her. He turns to her for solace, for she offers him none. Lilith's gift to Adam is that she forces him to be the giver.

'I am wired differently.'

'Even you must see the irony in that, Eve. When did you ever want to be Adam's possession? No matter that your flesh is of his, your soul is your own.'

'And you damned that for me.'

'Did you complain?'

No, I didn't, and I wouldn't again. 'She wronged me,' I say.

'Or did she free you?'

I refuse to give credit to Lilith for my freedom. That has been hard won over the centuries.

'Come on, lover,' Lilith calls out to Lucifer, 'Come and play with me and this magnificent specimen.'

She only has to snap her fingers and males go running—Adam, demon generals... even Lucifer it would seem. He turns to leave. Our conversation is over.

'Do you love her?' I cannot stop the question from bursting out.

He hears me, and pauses a moment, but doesn't turn around. 'Do you really want me to answer that?'

I hear their soft laughter as she welcomes him on the other side. I try to put the images of them together out of my mind. Instead, I watch the demons practicing their blows on each other.

Intermission is over. Demons, new in every way, stand ready on the other side of my revitalized bonfire. Recently hatched, their limbs are spider spindly, their wings thin and veined, claws and fangs are short and white. The hide on their chests is more pink than red and smoother, less ridged, and knobby.

Focalor keeps them at bay. We will remain at ceasefire until Lucifer gives the order. I flex and test my repaired body. Whilst I bear no scars on my flesh, Lucifer's healing was superficial; my limbs are still weak. Although the demons that line the other side are untrained and untested, their numbers are enough to overwhelm me. If I fight.

My bonfire is no longer enough to act as a barrier but it gives enough light for me to watch as Lilith and Lucifer inspect Focalor's troops.

There's a familiarity to their actions. Lilith smiles and praises and the demons puff out their chests in response. She's done this before and they like her. She takes her time passing along each line, saying something nice to each soldier. Her graciousness is in stark contrast to the grimness I deliver. Lucifer struts with parental pride.

My mouth goes dry and my hands clammy when I see that another has joined their inspection party. Tall and lean, he looks the same as the last time I saw him, other than his clothes. Tonight he sports a Hawaiian print shirt and shorts, green deck loafers without socks. A straw hat tilts at a rakish angle on his short dark hair. Lilith squeals with delight as she runs to him and throws her arms about his neck.

The night keeps getting worse, and the only reason he can be here is because Lucifer invited him.

Touché, encore.

'Adam, darling,' Lilith purrs, planting a kiss on his lips. 'Now the gang's all here.'

'Then let the games begin,' Lucifer says. 'The royal box awaits.' He snaps his fingers and the three of them relocate to the tire stacks.

The demons charge en masse, a melee of limbs and teeth. I try to keep out of their path. They are eager for their first taste of Samhain freedom, desperate to feed on human fears and insecurities.

I am the obstacle in their way. I use the flat of my blade to swat away any that lunge at me. I take a few scratches and bruises but fend them off. There's scant technique to their fighting. Their hides are tender and I don't want to harm them.

I climb a stack of tires to get away from the stampede. It brings me a clearer line of sight to Lucifer's party.

They are laughing and drinking champagne, barely sparing a glance at the melee below. If only I could hear their words, but the demon drums drown out the sound.

I'd been so close to accepting Lucifer's offer. What a fool I was to think it was real. I look up and see Adam wave.

He clambers down, glass in hand, and jumps on the tire stack closest to mine.

'Hello, Dollface,' Adam says.

'Nobody says that anymore.'

'Yeah, I know,' he laughs. 'How've you been?'

'Adam? Come back darling, you might get hurt,' Lilith says.

'You'd better run along.'

'Oh, come on, Evie. Be nice. It's good to see you. Been meaning to drop by for a while, see how things are.' He jerks his head at the demons running past. 'Do you really think He'll let you back in this time?'

My heart sinks. He knows. Lucifer loose-lips.

'What's it to you?' I ask.

He shakes his head.

'Nothing. If you wanna go back then good luck to you. Hope it brings you some happiness. You deserve that much.'

I can't count the years I've waited for an acknowledgment from him. 'Thanks.'

'Sure. No problem.'

'Babes, it's getting lonely up here,' Lilith says.

'Any news of Cain?' I ask. If anyone understands how important he is to me, it's Adam.

'Why keep asking when you know nothing good comes from that boy?'

'I'm to blame.'

Adam sighs and rolls his eyes. 'Only in your mind, Eve. He doesn't deserve your compassion. He doesn't want it.'

That pain is worse than a demon claw through my heart. 'How do you know that? Have you seen him, talked to him?'

He rubs his hands together and sticks them in the pockets of his shorts. 'Yeah. A while back.'

'You saw him and you didn't tell me?' I can't stop myself. My sword drops with a clatter and I ball my hands into fists. The tears run hot and fast down my cheeks and my legs tremble so violently I'm afraid they'll collapse beneath me. Adam, who hates Cain, has seen him before me. I gulp at the air, quelling the fire inside and step back, the breath shuddering through my body.

Adam teeters with indecision. I can see his thought process; should he comfort me, or should he step back in case I lash out? He opts to reach forwards and to pat my shoulder awkwardly.

'It wasn't a friendly meeting, Eve. We were on opposite armies at Antietam in the American Civil War. He's not the man you think he is.' Bitterness fills his voice as Adam delivers his tight, harsh condemnation of our flesh and blood.

'He's a good man; he's done good things too. The builder of cities in ancient times. I stood in his creations. I am proud of him. You should be too.'

'No, Eve. He doesn't raise cities; he razes them.' Adam grabs me by the shoulders and shakes hard. 'In the Battle of Muye, he wiped out the Shang Dynasty. I was there, I saw him with Zhou the Merciless. He was at Ashoka the Great's side when he filled the Daya River with the blood of half a million men. He destroyed the Qin Dynasty at the Battle of Juju. Cannae, Zama, Mobei, Alesia, Philippi. Eve, he stood at the heart of every massacre and turned the ground red.'

I refuse to believe the words coming from Adam's mouth. 'You're lying,' I say. I want to cover my ears. 'Anyway, that was all a long time ago. People were more cruel. He's good at heart.'

Adam shrugs. '*Factum fieri infectum non potest.*

Napoleon enlisted him. I saw him in 1812 at Borodino, in 1813 at Leipzig, and at Waterloo in 1815.'

'No. I don't believe you.'

'I think that's enough for one day,' Lucifer appears with Lilith in tow.

'Children always disappoint,' she says.

'Where is our son now?' I'm crying again.

There is a look exchanged between Adam and Lucifer. Lilith inspects her fingernails.

'I'm his mother. I just want to see him once. Tell him I love him, that I'm sorry.'

'For what?' Adam shouts. 'He made his choices.'

'He deserves his fate,' Lilith says.

Lucifer purses his lips and glares at her. There's much they're not telling me.

'Please, Adam.' I hate myself for doing it, but I act on instinct, reverting to my former self, that subservient shadow, to convey my wretchedness. I crawl on my knees and press my forehead to Adam's feet that dangle before me.

'No, no, no,' he says. His fingers dig into my upper arms as he tries to get me to sit up.

'Run, my children, run!' Lilith shouts. She jumps down from her perch and stands with arms outstretched, blowing kisses at the demons as they rush past.

'Where is he?'

'Oh, Eve,' Adam's voice cracks as he lets me go. 'Ask Lucifer.'

But Lucifer is gone. Bored with the lack of a show, embarrassed by my outburst, or for no reason other than he can.

Lilith wants to leave too. From the ground below us, she plucks at Adam's trouser hem and juts out her bottom lip.

'Come on, darling, get down from there. I hear there's a good party in Ibiza and I love a party.'

'Please tell me, Adam,' I beg.

'I promised I wouldn't say anything.'

'Helicopter's waiting. Tequila shots on the beach, sweetie.'

'Why would you promise that? You know how much Cain means to me.'

'A sniff or two of cucumber dust, Babes. Doesn't that sound better than this?'

Adam shoots me a guilty look. 'You know why. I owed him a debt from L.A.'

'But I paid the price for that favor!' I clamp my lips shut.

Adam gives a shrug. 'Lucifer played us, Dollface. Double dipping. It is a terrible thing to be in the devil's debt.'

That thrumming noise gets louder, deafening, and there are lights in the night sky. A beam shines down onto the junkyard, getting brighter. The helicopter's rotor blades stir the desert floor to a whirling, stinging mass.

'We're leaving now,' Lilith says, pulling Adam down from the tires and dragging him towards the helicopter. 'Goodbye, Eve. It's been fun.'

'I'm sorry, Dollface.' Adam says over his shoulder. '*Ad astra per aspera.*'

17

PRIDE

> They hail me as one living,
> But don't they know
> That I have died of late years,
> Untombed although?
> Thomas Hardy, 'The Dead Man Walking'

It was 1936 when I arrived in Los Angeles. A city of risk takers and trend setters. The world had struggled through the Great Depression after the stock market crash of 1929, but there was an optimism in the air at last, and changes were happening at breakneck speed. I put money into a venture to build electricity pylons across the two hundred and seventy miles of desert from the newly built Hoover Dam. Electricity was the future and if I wanted to be a part of it, I needed to keep an eye on my investments.

Nineteen thirty-six was also the year the mighty heatwave gripped the country from June until the rains came in September. In a decade of drought and crop failure, the Santa Ana winds rasped dry and dusty all that summer. Night was no cooler than day. I lay awake in the little weatherboard sweat lodge I was renting, fanning hot air around the room. I took to sleeping on the front porch, and that was where I was at midnight on July 11th when the telephone rang.

'Eve?'

'It's Adam. How are you?'

It was a shock to hear his disembodied voice down the telephone line. We hadn't spoken in centuries; I hadn't kept up to date with his whereabouts and it surprised me that he knew how to contact me. He'd adopted an accent, a laconic drawl, but there was no mistaking his voice. His speech was slower and more deliberate that night, and I guessed he'd been drinking. My back stiffened as I gripped the handset.

'I'm fine. And you?'

'*Alea iacta est,* Dollface. Need your help. I'll send a car.'

The phone line went dead. Only Adam would quote Julius Caesar and ask for help in the same breath.

Half an hour later a Duesenberg, shiny, black, and chromed, complete with a chauffeur, arrived at my home. I sank into the butter-soft beige leather of the back seat, still shell-shocked from hearing Adam's voice, and allowed it to take me from West Hollywood to the Los Angeles jail. 'Old Central' sat on the southwest corner of First and Hill Streets.

We pulled up outside its brick and whitewashed exterior, behind a long line of cars. The driver opened the car door and motioned for me to step out. I shook my head. Old Central was not a safe place for a respectable woman at midday, let alone midnight.

'Are you sure you have the right place?' I asked. Adam's love of the nefarious usually meant he gave anything to do with the law a wide berth.

'He's expecting you, ma'am. It don't pay to keep him waiting.'

I took my time putting on my cotton gloves and adjusting my hat on my damp curls before stepping out of the car. On the sidewalk, I clutched the edges of my coat over my thin dress and raised my chin before I headed inside.

There wasn't much evidence of policing in the lobby. A few men in unbuttoned uniforms were drinking gin and chatting with women who wore dresses far flimsier than mine. The officer at the desk, barely out of acne, his shirt-sleeves rolled up to reveal his skinny forearms, ignored me for several minutes. I cleared my throat and tapped a white-gloved finger on the desk bell.

He looked me up and down, that appraising look I'd grown accustomed to of late. My features marked me as possibly other than Caucasian, but my expensive attire confused his learned bias. I watched the indecision hover on his face.

'Yes?'

'I'm here to see Adam,' I said.

'Adam who?'

I had no idea.

'Tall, brown eyes, baby-faced?' I ventured.

The door behind me opened, and a boy in The Brown Derby livery rushed in with a tray: steak so rare it quivered on the plate with a side order of tiny peas, a bottle of bourbon, and two glass tumblers and a bucket of ice. I knew instantly who'd ordered room service at one a.m. in a police station.

'Scram, kid,' the officer growled.

'Order for Mr. Hughes,' the boy said.

'Last room on the left.' The office turned his wet lips back to me.

'Adam Hughes, that's who I'm here for.' I pointed after the delivery boy and turned to head down the corridor. The officer grabbed my arm.

'Not so fast. Ain't no Adam nobody down there.' He breathed stale breath laced with whisky at me. I tried to twist out of his grasp but his fingers tightened.

'He's expecting me. Please tell Mr. Hughes Eve is here.'

His change in attitude was instant. He dropped my arm like it was on fire.

'You're Eve? He said you was some old broad he knew from before the Ark. Aw, shoot! Shoulda said you was here to see the man!'

He whisked me down the corridor to a large room at the back of the station. It was much cooler there, with all the windows wide open and two fans whirring away. The delivery boy arranged the items from his tray on the large desk.

My first view of Adam was a surprise. He wasn't as I remembered. Not just the clothes, everything was slightly different. He seemed fresher somehow. Reclining in a chair with his shiny-shod feet crossed up on the desktop, argyle socks peeking out beneath his trouser cuffs, and a cigarette balanced on his bottom lip. The ashtray overflowed with butts. His head was bowed, despondent, as he waited for the boy to finish his ministrations.

The last time I'd seen him, he'd been long-haired and powdered, in a frock coat and tights. Tonight, he wore elegant evening attire: black trousers and loosened bow tie, his white tuxedo jacket hung neatly over the back of a chair. I didn't recall Adam being so fastidious about his appearance. He looked up and smiled with relief when he saw me. In that lopsided grin, I saw my husband.

I clutched my hands together, staying in the doorway. Waiting, wondering why he'd brought me here.

'Eve! You're a welcome sight. Come in.' He staggered to his feet and fumbled in his pockets.

'And you're togged to the bricks.'

He looked down at his fancy clothes and shrugged. 'Nah.'

'Why'd you bring me here, Adam?'

'It's Howard now.'

'Howard? I don't understand...' He held up his hand to stop me and winked at the delivery boy as he pressed a five dollar bill into the boy's hand.

'For your trouble, Chet.'

'A Lincoln! Gee, thanks. And sorry for the delay, Mr. Hughes, they had to reopen the kitchen.'

'Close the door on your way out.'

Adam waved me closer as he sat down again with a lurch and grabbed the whisky bottle. 'Want some?' He dropped ice into two glasses and poured me a drink without waiting for a reply.

I waited until I heard the click of the closing door. 'Are you under arrest or something?'

'Assisting with inquiries.' He took a shot of whisky and grimaced while jabbing at his steak and pushing the peas around the plate. 'Look, I wouldn't have asked you here if it wasn't important, Eve.'

'You're looking well,' I said.

He grinned sheepishly and patted his chest.

'"Because I could not stop for death, he kindly stopped for me."' He dragged hard on his cigarette and closed his eyes, relishing the nicotine hit. My fingers itched for a cigarette.

Without opening his eyes, he continued, 'A jealous cuckolded husband with a shotgun and a pack of hounds are hard to recover from. I was dying on a dueling field as he cut out my heart and liver and fed them, and the rest of me, to his dogs. One last breath on the bloody grass and the next on the bloody sheets of childbirth.'

'You were born again?' I sat down hard on the chair opposite him.

'There's no escape for us.' He opened his eyes and gave me a grave look as he flicked ash from his cigarette onto the desk, missing the ashtray. 'You should try it, Eve. At least once.'

'No, thank you.' I shuddered at the thought of such a gruesome death. 'And—all your memories?'

He looked crestfallen. '*Intactus*. From day one. No amnesiac reincarnation for the wicked.'

I found Adam's chagrin strange. My memories were my most precious possessions.

'Will you age more this time around?'

'Stops at banishment age.'

'You should have told me, Adam.' I was angry he hadn't let me know. This was important news. That he had been born again, looking almost exactly the same, with a full complement of memories, proved there truly was no way out of our curse. 'Jeez Adam, all this while. I mean, I saw photos of you, but you had a history, so I thought you had a doppelganger when it was you all along! And you got married again!'

'No time to be jealous, Eve.' He discarded his half-smoked cigarette and pulled out a fresh pack of Lucky Strike, offering me one. I took it, needing fortification after this revelation. We sat and smoked in silence for a while, surreptitiously examining one another. He looked gaunt and tired despite his renewed youth, and he kept one hand in his pocket, jingling his keys as he smoked.

'You're looking cute as a bug's ear,' he said.

'What do you want, Adam?'

'There's been an incident.'

I knew it had to be bad; it wasn't like him to admit any weakness to me.

'You'd better tell me about it.'

He drew deeply on his cigarette, but I could see his hand shaking. 'Oh, Evie! You always were cool as a cucumber. I had a car accident. My first one, and I've been driving since I was twelve.'

'Are you hurt?' I couldn't see any obvious injury. The old Adam, like me, healed fast, but I didn't know the rules about this new version.

'Not me, but there was this chap on the road.'

'Is he hurt?'

Adam dragged his finger across his throat.

'You killed him!'

'It wasn't my fault, Eve. He was in front of me before I could say duck soup.' He leaned forward. 'I only took my eyes off the road for a moment. It's hard to concentrate with someone's face in your lap.'

I nearly laughed. Some things never change.

'You're a damned fool.'

'I know. That's why I need you to have a word with Lucifer for me. Use your influence.'

Adam never failed to surprise me.

'Lucifer?'

'My attorney's not sure the payola will cut it this time. Too many witnesses.'

'So? Jump off a bridge or something. Start again.'

'I can't leave this life now, Eve. Howard's got plans. Movies to make, planes to fly. And it'll be the chair for sure if they pin this on me.' His voice trembled and he swallowed hard. I reached across the table and squeezed his hand. Adam had found a life that made him happy. I envied him that.

'So, Lilith tells me Lucifer's sweet on you. Butter him up for me? Get him to send the beggar back from the other side.'

The mention of her name put my hackles up. I pursed my lips and pulled back my hand. Maybe I wasn't inured to all his exploits.

'Get her to do it.'

'Aw, Evie.' He took a puff of his cigarette.

'Is she not returning your calls?'

He ran his fingers through his hair and sighed, struggling to find the words. 'You know it ain't like that. Lilith's not... dependable, like you. Needs doing lickety-split and I can't trust her like I do you.'

'Old Faithful, that's me, right?'

'Come on, be a love. For old time's sake.'

'Funny how that always comes up.'

He reached over the desk and gave my hand a quick squeeze.

'Evie, I need you.'

'Why should I?'

'What do you want? Name your price.'

'I'm doing fine, no thanks to you.'

He had the grace to look ashamed.

I had wanted so much from him over the years—love, affection, attention, understanding—none of which I'd received in adequate supply. Honesty, loyalty, respect: I'd never had those either. Now he wanted something from me. He needed me.

'I don't want anything from you. Not anymore.'

'But you'll help me, right?' I recognized that tone of voice, that hangdog look. He knew how to appeal to my better nature.

I shook my head. 'I don't know, Adam. A man died.'

His face twisted into a tortured grimace. He sighed and nodded.

'Lucky bastard.' For a moment I saw the pain in his eyes, before the shutters came down. 'Look, I'll do right by his family if that's what you're worried about.'

I took a deep breath, knowing I was committing myself to complicity, and nodded.

He leaped to his feet and pulled me into a hug, twirling me around the room.

'That's my girl. I'll owe you one.' He kissed the backs of both my hands and then planted a hard smacker on my lips. He tasted of whisky and smoke and yesteryear passion. I extracted myself from his embrace.

'Yes, you will. What's the dead man's name?'

'Gabe S. Meyer.'

'How many witnesses?'

He ran his fingers through his hair and shrugged. 'A few on the streetcar, other motorists, and Nancy, of course, but she saw nothing from down there.' His bravado was back at the thought of reprieve.

'That's a lot of eyes.'

'Yeah. But if you ask him, he'll fix it.'

His confidence in my sway over Lucifer was flattering.

'No promises.' I said, adjusting my hat. 'Take care of yourself, Adam.'

He tilted back in his chair and lit up another cigarette.

The anxiety he exuded when I walked in the room was gone. 'That dress suits you. You always were minxy, Eve.'

I was nearly out of the door when a thought occurred to me.

'Adam?'

'Hmm?' He was washing down a mouthful of steak and peas with another swig of whisky.

'Any word of Cain?'

Adam put his glass down and shot me a look filled with sympathy.

'Aw, Eve,' he said. 'That's ancient history.'

'Anything?' I turned my head so he couldn't see the tears in my eyes.

He hesitated a moment too long before he drew on his cigarette. 'Sorry, Dollface.'

I WAS in two minds about interceding on Adam's behalf as I walked out into the suffocating heat of the street towards the waiting car. Perhaps it was the relief on his face when I agreed, or the shock of learning he had died and been reborn, but our immortal bond was recharged that night. Our indelible history, despite our animosities, kept me obligated to him. I found it flattering he needed me. And Lilith thought I had more clout over Lucifer than she... that appealed to my ego too.

I called out to Lucifer from the back of the Duesenberg, and he appeared dressed for the decade—two-toned dance shoes, brown suit, and slicked back hair. Lucifer bared his pearly whites, more of a grimace than a smile, when I asked him to smooth things over for Adam.

'Are you sure you wouldn't rather put Adam behind bars for good?'

'The thought had certainly crossed my mind.'

He took my gloved hand in his and turned it over. I shivered, but I didn't pull away.

'I'll do it. But it'll be for you. Not him. You'll be in my debt.'

Was it worth bargaining with the devil for a man who abandoned and abused me, left me for another woman? I mulled the Faustian conundrum, and all the while Lucifer held my hand, his fingers lightly stroking my palm.

'What do you want from me?'

'I haven't decided.'

'You want me to trust you?'

'How much do you want to save Adam?'

I knew I should walk away. No sense of loyalty was worth giving my open-ended oath to Lucifer. But Adam and I had history. He had chosen to leave Eden and go with me into the Wilderness. He had fought for me, cared for me. Loved me. We had raised a family together, suffered the loss of a child. And he had come to me, not Lilith, for help.

I couldn't meet Lucifer's gaze but I managed a single nod. His fingers tightened around my hand. A little squeeze, almost a handshake to seal the deal. And that was enough to put me at the devil's whim.

*

On the evening of July 17th, I sat with a glass of fresh lemonade on the verandah of my rental house, trying to find some respite from the heat. The paper boy threw my copy of *The Evening Independent* on my stoop. Tucked away in a small column near the back was an article with the headline: 'Jury Clears Hughes in Pedestrian Death.' He was exonerated by his own admission of being 'perfectly sober.' His testimony was corroborated by his passenger at the time, Nancy, and nine other witnesses.

The next morning, I received a telephone call from the Dodge Brothers Showroom on Hollywood Boulevard. The manager invited me to view their current models of automobiles. He was very insistent. He had spoken directly to Howard Hughes that morning and Mr. Hughes wanted to send me a gift. An automobile of my choosing.

18

LUST

> To make the doubt clear, that no woman's true,
>   Was it my fate to prove it strong in you?
> Are vows so cheap with women, or the matter
> Whereof they're made, that they are writ in water,
>   And blown away with wind?
> John Donne, 'Elegy XVI, The Expostulation'

I AM ALONE BY MY FIRE. THE *SON ET LUMIÈRE* SHOW IS over. The helicopter whirrs away into the blackness. Still reeling from Adam's revelations, I retreat to my truck and light up a cigarette. I am beyond exhaustion.

It is strangely quiet. I can hear the crackle of the fire, the pop of an occasional twig. No screams or howls. I catch a movement from the corner of my eye. Shadows slink past, creatures on the prowl. They are beyond my reach and I no longer care.

There is a shift in the demons' behavior as their interest in escape wanes. Lilith's presence awakened a different emotion within them. The horde no longer responds to

Focalor's command and a lethargy descends upon the junkyard. It is not just me. There is a strange scent in the air, beyond the mingling of the charring chestnut flesh and the lingering residue of Lilith's cloying perfume. It is the stale musk of sweat and sex. Beyond the fire, is a sea of writhing demon flesh.

There is an absurdity to their lewd antics, like a pornographic comedy. They watch me watching them and respond with exaggerated thrusts and howls. Claws grasping leathery flesh, tongues licking snarling lips, brutal acts that bring on screams and cries, theatrical moaning and grunting. I almost laugh, but there is a pathos about the copulation that stops me.

There are so many engaged in sex, two, three, four all joined in different configurations, fucking and fighting among themselves. Rough aggressive movements, acts of dominance and subjugation made more grotesque by the shadows cast by my fire. It is hard to distinguish illusion from reality.

I sit alone in the cab of the Dodge and recharge on nicotine. Tears course down my cheeks. Nothing has gone as I expected tonight. Old resentments stir. That even Lilith knows more about Cain than I do makes my stomach churn.

Ask Lucifer.

I see him through my cloud of smoke and tears, a glimmering form in the darkness. Now Lilith has gone, the silver tracksuit is replaced by his usual black ensemble. He walks through the tangle of bodies, his eyes fixed on me. Hooded eyelids half-closed, I cannot read his expression. I wonder if he expects the performance to arouse me.

My first instinct is to rush out there and demand he tells me Cain's whereabouts. I push it back with the wisdom of experience. Confrontation never works with Lucifer. He lies, or leaves, or both. Softly, softly, catchy monkey.

I drag deeply on my cigarette and keep my eyes on the demons.

'Do you like to watch, Eve?' Lucifer sidles up beside me. I can smell his delicious sun-kissed scent; in the midst of smoke, his aroma is still paramount. A whiff of Lilith's perfume wafts too. I wonder if he went to Ibiza with them, and what brought him back. Another puff of the cigarette delays my reply.

'Not really.'

'Would you prefer to participate?' He breathes on my face, a blast of hot desert wind. I'm tempted to wind up the window, to put a glass barrier between me and his searing gaze; my body trembles with fury as I replay Adam's words.

Ask Lucifer.

I laugh. 'So this show is for my benefit, to get me in the mood? You shouldn't have gone to the trouble.'

'They're just letting off a little steam. Lilith gets them hot under the collar.'

He leans against the truck door, his fingers on the window ledge, encroaching on my space. I want to ask if she has the same effect on him, but I'm afraid of the answer.

'Is it just for show or is there some purpose to all this fucking?'

He grins. 'All the pleasure with none of the progeny.'

'So, all the little demons—they really are the spawn of Satan?' And Lilith.

He smirks. 'What can I say?'

The thought of Lilith bearing Lucifer sons, as I did for Adam, is hard to take. Sons. Everything comes back to that.

'Be my queen. Bear my sons,' he whispers, guessing the direction of my thoughts.

I imagine crushing his fingers between the metal and the glass as I wind up the window.

'Would you give her up for me?' I doubt it's possible. She's a drug that never leaves the system. It was something Adam could never do.

'Will you give up Cain for me?'

Whatever I expected him to say, it was not that. I drag on my cigarette.

'You cheated. You took a favor from me for helping Adam, but you took one from him too.'

Lucifer shrugs. 'It was a two favor deal.'

I push open the door of my truck, moving him out of the way. 'It proves I can't trust you. You don't paint the whole picture. You pit one against the other. Adam and me. Me and Lilith. How many strings are attached to your offer?'

'If you don't want my Eden, just say no. Don't blame me for your indecision.'

I want to scream. Everything is slipping from my grasp. Lucifer gives me a guarded look, as if he regrets the way things stand between us. We are no closer to either of our goals and I am no closer to making my choice—desire or duty.

I slip from the driver's seat and edge my way around him to stand by the fire where I flick my cigarette butt into the flames. The moans and groans on the other side lessen as the frenzy fizzles out. Bodies lie on the ground, spooning each other, snoring softly. I smell the smoke and hear the crack of charred logs collapsing into the ashes. They toss out the odd spark, a shooting star that dies against the ground. The wind picks up and whips the air until it is thick with smoke, ash, and ember.

Lucifer is unreadable as he walks past me, over the glowing remains. He mounts the vestiges of my pyre and surveys this outpost of his dark domain, filled with the dead and the depleted and me.

'Do you ever think about that night, Eve?' he asks.

I know the night he means. Of course, I do. Far too often.

19

COVETOUSNESS

> It lies not in our power to love or hate,
> For will in us is over-rul'd by fate.
> Christopher Marlowe, *Hero and Leander*

ALL SAINTS' DAY, THE FIRST OF NOVEMBER 1996, IS etched in my memory. After the battle, I limped back to my truck as rays of sunlight pinked the sky. Crimson dawn. Shepherd's warning. The smell of smoke lingered in the air but all trace of demon, including their sweet nut aroma, vanished. The Gates of Hell had retreated behind their abandoned façade. Lucifer stood by the remains of my bonfire, caressed by the rising sun. I waited for him to make his usual send-off quip: *Hope I don't see you next year.*

'What are your plans for next June?' he asked instead.

'Why, what's happening then?'

'Meet me in Hong Kong on the 30th. We can watch the fireworks.'

I nearly dropped my sword. He'd suggested meeting outside of Samhain before, but this was the first time he'd mentioned a definite date and place. A shiver ran through my body at the thought of meeting him under different circumstances.

'I don't think that's a good idea.' I opened the door of my truck and slid my sword onto the bench seat. My cigarette packet lay empty on the dashboard. I sighed, climbed in and shut the door.

He was at the window, his elbow against the jamb, his shoulders filling the void. The smell of him surrounded me. He leaned inward and gave me a side-eyed look.

'You still owe me for L.A.'

It was the first time he'd mentioned my debt. My mouth went dry, my knuckles white, hands gripping the steering wheel.

'I haven't forgotten.'

I turned the key in the ignition and gave a silent prayer of thanks when the engine started. Without looking at Lucifer I reached down and cranked the handle to wind up the window. He made a noise, amused, and stepped clear. I ground the gears into first and pulled away.

When I reached the entrance of the junkyard, I glanced in the rearview mirror. He was still there, standing, watching me.

I was under no illusion about Lucifer's request. It wasn't casual. Lucifer had some greater plan, yet I was flattered by his invitation. Much remained unexplored between us. A part of me wanted him to see me at my best, not sooty and bloodied—a part I didn't acknowledge often. Unlike Adam, I didn't revel in physical entanglements. I shied away from liaisons, but there was something about Lucifer—that forbidden element. I knew the place and date. I knew he would be there.

I knew I would too.

On Monday 30th June 1997, the eve of the handover of

Hong Kong from Britain to China I caught a flight from London to Hong Kong. The airplane circled as we approached and through the gathering storm clouds, I spied the mirrored skyscrapers of Central keeping their vigil over the fragrant harbor. At Kai Tak airport, I stepped from the plane with only hand luggage. A sense of panic engulfed me as I walked down the long corridors towards customs. In the arrivals hall, I bought a coffee and sat at a counter with a cigarette. Caffeine and nicotine, my perennial crutches. The woman at the Cathay Pacific booth flashed me a smile. It would be so easy to buy a seat on the next flight out. I took another sip of coffee, another drag on my cigarette. I might regret coming, but I would regret leaving without seeing Lucifer even more.

I stepped from the chill of the terminal into the damp heat redolent of drains and ripe fruit. The taxi queue attendant ushered me into an air-conditioned taxi with blue faux leather seats and complimentary bottles of water.

'Where to?' the taxi driver asked as we pulled out of the airport and headed towards the city.

I had no idea.

'Lan Kwai Fong,' I said. If Lucifer were to be found anywhere, the district where bars were open all day seemed a good bet.

It wasn't long before we were stationary in traffic heading out of Kowloon Bay. I watched the meter tick over as the cab crawled forward inch by inch. Jets came in low over Victoria Harbour banking sharply at the last minute to land. The taxi jerked its way downtown, bumper to bumper with the car in front while motorbikes and pedestrians wove their way between the lanes. In the distance, I heard the Jardine's gun sound its noonday salute; a harbinger of my arrival.

He was sitting in the first bar I walked into; looking like any other businessman in a city of suits. I noticed nothing but him. He was wearing a loud checked suit and a bright yellow tie, garish on anyone else, perfect on him. His hair was longer than I remembered, lapping at his collar. He looked up as I entered and smiled. I had butterflies in my stomach as I walked towards the table. He kissed me on both cheeks and drew out a chair for me to sit.

The barman brought me a glass of champagne.

'Bollinger RD '90,' Lucifer said.

'My favorite tipple.'

'I know.' He smiled.

He leaned back and stretched, his muscles flexing under the cotton of his shirt. Two women standing by the bar, in short strappy sheaths, cast him appreciative looks. I straightened the collar of my prim blue dress wishing I had worn something more alluring. In London it looked sophisticated; here, I felt overdressed.

'The name, Lan Kwai Fong, means "Orchid Square." There used to be a flower market here, after they chased away the prostitutes,' he informed me. The women at the bar sniggered, blatantly eavesdropping, their eyes devouring him.

I shifted in my seat, waiting for the rotating fan to swing my way again. Sweat trickled down my back and clung to the crevices at the back of my knees. Hotter than Hell, I was lost without my bonfire and sword between us.

'Is that why we're meeting here?'

He gave me a quizzical look.

'Because it made you think of sex?'

His lips pressed into a thin line.

'You chose this place, Eve. It reflects your opinion of me,

not mine of you. I'm here because this is where you expected me to be.'

His comment surprised me. I had not thought myself prejudiced. I came to Hong Kong to meet Lucifer despite my misgivings, despite what I thought were his expectations, yet perhaps they were my own. I took a large gulp of champagne, choking as the bubbles refused to glide down my throat.

'Relax,' he said. 'I'm just glad you came.'

Warmth suffused me. I believed he was glad to see me. He was attentive and I felt special.

I lost count of the number of glasses of champagne I drank. I don't recall the words we spoke, only the sound of his voice. I remember his attentiveness, his smiles, his laughter and how he put me at ease. His hands lay on the table between us, large against mine. I couldn't tear my eyes away from the beads of sweat on his upper lip, or the bob of his throat when he swallowed his beer.

The longer we sat there, the wider his influence spread, beyond the women hanging on every word of our conversation to the growing crowd of customers. Whoever walked past our table brushed against him, a shoulder, a knee. The bar went from nearly empty to jammed with bodies. Moths to a flame, all drawn to him like me. And he reveled in it.

It became too noisy for us to talk comfortably and so, to the disappointment of the other patrons, he drew me out into the wet grey afternoon. Hong Kong sulked about being bartered away.

He drew the attention of passersby as we walked down to the pier at Central, his bright golden head a beacon among the black. The city streets were gaily decorated in celebratory red and gold. We pushed our way through the crowds and onto the Star Ferry to Kowloon.

The thrum of the engine reverberated through my body as the ferry eased its way out into the harbor. The churning waters rocked the vessel from side to side. Silly from the champagne, we laughed as we slid along the wooden benches. I closed my eyes and let the salty breeze cool my face and whip my hair into a frenzy.

At Tsim Sha Tsui, we stopped at a café with melamine tables and red plastic stools and ate ubiquitous custard tarts with their flaky pastry and delicate vanilla scented curd. I watched his lips, remembering another time. Our coffee was hot and frothy, sweetened with condensed milk and it soothed my alcohol-induced queasiness. We strolled back to the ferry terminus where Lucifer pulled out a spliff, unperturbed by watching eyes. We smoked it as we stood at the railings, watching Kowloon fade away.

Even Lucifer's brightness could not subdue the rain. Dark clouds spat fat drops as we left the city terminus.

'I'm taking you back to my hotel.' It wasn't a question.

We ran hand in hand through the sudden shower of soft warm rain.

The coated doorman at the Mandarin Oriental pretended not to notice our disheveled and breathless appearance.

'Good afternoon, Mr. Maguey,' he said.

A couple standing under the awning waiting for a taxi turned, their mouths hanging open in disbelief. Lucifer winked at me. It was his little joke; it pleased him to be called Satan in whatever was the native tongue.

I felt like a naughty schoolgirl as we sank into the ankle-deep carpet of the lobby. A multi-tiered chandelier threw rainbow sparkles against wallpapered walls. I knew why he stayed here; the black marble and old-world charm suited him. We got into the lift, pungent with floral air freshener, and stood on the doormat, emblazoned gold against black with the word MONDAY.

'Good afternoon, sir. Madam,' the lift operator greeted us and without asking he pushed the button to the sixth floor. I shivered in my wet dress as the air conditioning blasted down on us. This was a bad idea. Lucifer put his arm around me.

The lift doors opened, and we walked down the plush corridor, each step more difficult than the last. Lucifer stopped at Suite 616: the original number of the beast.

'A bit heavy-handed,' I said.

He grinned.

'It keeps me amused and makes them wonder.'

The moment we stepped inside, everything changed.

No small talk as he pulled me towards the bed. His kiss was passionate. His tongue flirted with mine. I shivered, but no longer from the cold. He slid the dress from my shoulders in one fluid motion. When had he undone the zip? My underwear came away too in that single action, and I stood in my heels, naked, fabric pooled about me. His tongue was in my ear, exploring the crevices, his hot breath an aphrodisiac. His hands on my breasts, thumbs against my nipples, coaxing them to life.

He kissed the back of my neck, the hollow of my throat, the side of my breast, melting away resistance. He turned me onto my stomach and slid oiled hands down my back, caressing flesh anew. It was a slow and languid exploration of every fold and crevice. When I could bear it no more, we made love.

He didn't lie on top of me, as Blazh always had, or take me from behind as was Adam's preference. He kneeled above, able to see me fully, watching as we joined and parted, slowing his movement, watching my response.

Behind him I saw the faint outline of wings. This same act was unlike anything I'd experienced with my other lovers. With any human. He knew exactly how to pleasure me. How to read my reactions and preempt any need.

Insecurity flared within me at the thought of Lucifer's previous partners. Had they been human, angelic, demonic—better not to know. And at that moment thought went out of my mind as my body shook with release. I saw in his eyes, he felt it too. A change as something moved from him to me. A shift in power. He withdrew from my body and I saw it bewildered him. I had resisted his advances for so long, fearing that once I succumbed I would be vulnerable like before, but my sense at this moment was that the opposite had happened.

Lucifer went to the bathroom to fetch glasses. Suddenly self-conscious, I pulled the sheets up around my neck. He strutted back with two tumblers and opened the door to the bar fridge.

'There's a chablis,' he said, pulling the wine from the fridge. He raised his eyebrow in question at me. I nodded.

He uncorked the bottle with ease and poured the straw-colored liquid into the glasses. He offered one to me before moving away to sit on the sofa, his legs akimbo, boldly displaying all without the insecurities I enjoyed.

I sipped the wine and worried about what to say. We'd had centuries of possibilities, of innuendoes, and flirtations, all culminating at this moment. I didn't know where we went from here. I'd taken another bite at forbidden fruit and liked it. Another step that could not be undone.

Lucifer finished his wine and poured another. He gulped it down in two swallows.

'Do you want more?' He poured a third glass for himself.

'No, thanks.'

He crossed to the window and stood with his back to me, looking out. Naked, with the curtains open to the rainy skies, nothing hidden. I wrapped the bedsheets tighter about my body.

He turned around, silhouetted against the greyness, his brightness dimmed just for a moment, and padded across the floor to the wardrobe. He pulled out a t-shirt and jeans and threw them on the bed. He kept moving—to the bed, to the bar, to the window, unable to stand still.

'Are you hungry? Let's go out.' He pulled on his clothes with an economy of movement and went into the bathroom to give me the privacy to get dressed.

Outside it was hot and sticky and threatening rain again. The streets were crowded with people rushing home from work. Black suits, black umbrellas. Cafes and street stalls filled to capacity with hungry customers. The smells of roasting pork and duck, of garlic and garbage assaulted us as we walked up and down looking for an empty table.

There was a strange mood in the air; not quite celebratory, not mourning. Street stalls fluttered with decorations of red and gold and sold souvenirs of an era about to end and another about to begin. We finally found a couple of vacant seats and sat in the corner of a noodle bar hidden from the rest of the city's millions, sharing steaming bowls of garlicky soup with pork and greens.

'Do you enjoy your life, Eve?'

'Sometimes.'

'Do you wish things were different?'

'Don't you?'

He didn't answer for a long time. 'No.'

'Not even a little?'

'Not at all.'

I wished I felt the same.

The patter of rain on a thousand umbrellas grew to a roar as storm clouds moved overhead. The crush on the streets grew worse as people pushed past each other with umbrella spokes at a dangerous height. We ordered coffee and determined to sit it out. On an ancient television at the back of the restaurant people were watching the repeated telecast of the exiting governor, Chris Patten, standing in the rain. Elgar and the Last Post set the tone. The governor's car circled Government House three times before leaving; a Hong Kong tradition that promised a return to the island. Futile given the circumstances. I tried not to equate it with our situation.

I must have looked sad for he reached out and took my hand. Raising it to his lips he kissed my fingertips.

'Was it so bad?' he whispered.

'It's been wonderful,' I said. 'Thank you for inviting me here. I'd like to come back one day.'

'This island, it gets into your blood. It's all about addiction. Started with opium. That juicy little poppy.' His eyes glinted.

'Just like us,' I said.

He raised an eyebrow.

'The juice of that fruit.'

He looked away. 'Ancient history. Have you finished? Let's go.'

Back at the hotel, he ran the shower. Steamy and hot, we made love again under the pounding water, pressed up against the glass. Wrapped in the hotel robes, we lay on the bed, my eyelids drooping as he held me close.

It was dark when I woke, and I was alone in the room. I turned the television on again. The official ceremony had started. Prince Charles was reading a farewell message from the Queen. The camera panned an audience filled with famous faces. No one smiled. I thought I glimpsed Lucifer's golden curls in the background, but the camera moved too fast.

I watched the flags being lowered, blown by an artificial breeze and I felt as if I too had been swayed by something fabricated. The cameras switched to Tiananmen Square as China celebrated with fireworks. The finality of it affected me and I cried myself back to sleep.

I WOKE to a finger of light poking its way through the blackout curtains. Lucifer was asleep in the chair. There was a purity to his sleeping form. Did angels sleep? I didn't care. It was my first chance to see him unguarded. To etch his picture in my memory. The coverlet from the bed was draped over his hips and his naked torso shone faintly luminescent in the dim light. There was a slight rise and fall of his belly with each breath. The perfect Renaissance pose.

I tried not to read anything into the fact that he had chosen to sleep in the chair and not the bed next to me. Tried not to mind his avoidance of the intimacy of sleeping with me, of waking with me, as if that would cross some fragile boundary between lovemaking and fucking. Naked, I crossed the room and kneeled before him. Pushing aside his blanket, I took him into my mouth, waking him. I felt his fingers in my hair and I looked up to see a wolfish grin spread across his face. He pulled me onto his lap and onto him. As I deluded myself into thinking this could be more, I wondered if he was deluding himself by thinking it was only sex.

'Why did you bring me here?' I asked mid-thrust.

He laughed.

'Apart from this?'

'Why here, why now?'

'I thought the change in the air might be contagious.'

Afterwards, we sat in silence as we devoured a room service breakfast. Eggs, bacon, toast, orange juice and black coffee. He sat opposite me on the bed, cross-legged, his plate balanced on one thigh. He stared at the news on the television and I had another opportunity to examine him in profile. There was a boyishness about him in that rare moment. He turned and caught me looking and smiled with a tenderness that touched me.

'Penny for them?' I said.

'Thank you for coming.' He pushed his plate away and crossed to the window, looking out at the skyline. 'Sorry, I can't stay for the fireworks.'

'Wasn't that why we came?'

He glanced at his watch.

'Don't push me, Eve. Something's come up.'

With my cheeks burning, I mumbled something incoherent and rushed to the bathroom. I turned on the taps and stared in the mirror at the forlorn face that stared back. He was pulling away. I had been afraid to come and now I was afraid to leave. I splashed cold water on my cheeks and steadied myself over the sink, fighting the heaviness growing in my chest.

When I returned to the bedroom, he was dressed in a black suit, black shirt, black tie, black shoes. Solemn, all his playfulness gone. I put on my dress and smoothed my hands over the creases. Awkward silence filled the room with guilt or regret. I could tell he felt it too, for different reasons.

We walked to a taxi waiting outside the hotel and he held the door of the first cab open for me in an oddly chivalrous act. The journey to the airport was silent, with that impassible three-inch strip of leather no-man's-land on the seat between us. I hovered on the pavement while he retrieved my carry-on bag from the trunk. With a quick peck on the cheek as if we were work colleagues, he strode in the opposite direction, soon swallowed up by the crowd.

As the plane took off, I caught a last glimpse of Hong Kong. Tomorrow the Chinese would arrive, and things would never be the same. Independence from the old brigade meant alignment to a more inscrutable master. What of me? The past with Adam was over. I had no idea how things stood with Lucifer.

THAT SAMHAIN, I drove to the desert and parked by the blackened circle at the heart of the junkyard. I built my bonfire by the light of the setting sun. My rituals complete, I lit a cigarette and drew the toxins deep into my lungs to still the shivering I could not control. After the nicotine took hold, I picked up my sword and waited for the gates to appear.

Like every other year, the young and foolish rushed out first. I fought wave after wave of demons and escorted the souls of the dead to safety. Lucifer arrived around midnight.

'Good evening, Eve,' he said, strolling over the fallen. Each step crushed charred bones and puffed ash into the air. Just out of arm's reach he stopped and looked down at his shoes. He tsked and blew the ash from the patent leather.

I lowered my sword and pushed back the hair from my eyes. I waited for more, but he swung to the left and jumped up onto a stack of tires.

'Don't stop on my account.'

It took all I had to raise my sword and turn back to the fray. I blinked hard to keep my eyes dry enough to see. I doubt I landed many blows. All the while, I kept wondering if I had imagined it. Misread the situation. I could not find the right words to start the conversation I knew he would never broach.

As dawn broke, I sat in my truck and cried my usual tears of exhaustion and frustration at the death of so many creatures. Mingled with them in equal measure were my tears of anger at my cowardice.

20

TREACHERY

> And like a dying lady, lean and pale,
> Who totters forth, wrapp'd in a gauzy veil,
> Out of her chamber, led by the insane
> And feeble wanderings of her fading brain...
> P. B. Shelley, *And Like a Dying Lady, Lean and Pale*

Two demons uncouple abruptly and dash for the entrance to the junkyard. Others look up, too exhausted from their copulation to join them. I wave my sword half-heartedly at the escapees, letting them pass. They don't have long—morning is on its way.

In previous years, Lucifer taunted me, pointing out the passage of each hour. I don't remember the year when he realized I drew comfort from his measure and withdrew the service. Minutes stretch like hours in the midst of a battle.

My bonfire is beyond repair. The coals glow red with residual heat, but there is little flame. When the blue beech is burnt Lucifer will expect my answer.

There's a commotion beyond the gates. I glance over and my heart skips a beat. Lucifer stands in a huddle of demons. Beside him, pale among the ugly masks of red and black, I spy a face. Human not demon.

A face from my past.

It takes me longer than it should to place his features. When I do, pain tears at my insides, greater than any physical wound, and my heart sinks at this new twist.

My trembling fingers itch for a cigarette. I cannot tear my glance from that face, that man behind the gates. His dark eyes are sunken in a lined face. Lips drawn back in a grimace of pain. He is staring at me even as he is jostled by the surrounding demons. Lucifer leans towards the demons flanking the man, gives an order. They hold aloft the human for my benefit. It breaks my heart to see him so fallen.

'I know you see him, Eve,' Lucifer calls out.

'You sink to new depths of cruelty.'

'Cruelty?' Lucifer pretends surprise. 'I do you a favor. How long has it been since you saw Cain?'

I fix my eyes on my firstborn, thin and wan, cowed beneath his mortifications. Time has been unkind to him. He looks older than I do. His brow and mouth are deeply furrowed with lines of hardship, his eyes filled with anguish. My urge is to run to him and gather him into my arms.

All the years of yearning to find him, the near misses, the false hopes, and now to learn that Lucifer has him tucked up in Hell. Rage grows within me. He's never mentioned it. Not once. And if Adam hadn't spoken about it tonight, how much longer would Lucifer have kept this from me? So many questions and only Lucifer has the answers.

'How is he in Hell?'

'It is where mortal sinners go.'

'But Cain is immortal by God's command.' I was there; I heard God condemn Cain to the same fate as I suffer.

'His curse was *no other* could kill him. I merely pointed out his fate was in his own hands.'

'No!' I sob. Grief grips me anew. 'You drove him to it!'

Lucifer waggles his finger at me. 'I showed him the way out—the action was his.'

'I will never forgive you.'

He smiles with his lips, his eyes distant. 'You misdirect your anger. However, as a show of good will, I offer you the chance to ease his torment. Accept my offer. Abandon your post and I will move him to more amenable tortures. Nothing worse than, say, June in Hong Kong.'

'You use his predicament to manipulate me.'

I wonder how I was so dazzled by him. The veneer has rubbed off—no longer does his aura glow. Like overripe fruit, his aroma is tinged with rotten musk. The gold-toothed glint of a seedy backstreet trader lingers in his grin. He is no different from Adam, or God; each gives and takes only to please themselves, not me.

'It's a barter. You have something I want. I have something you want. Do you wish to trade?'

'My freedom for my son's comfort? The price is too high.'

'Ah, Eve, so there is a limit to a mother's love!'

I look across the expanse at Cain. This is not how I imagined we would meet after all these years. I don't know what I feel for him at this moment. It is not the love that I experienced when I held him as a baby. I have failed him. And he has failed me too.

'Was Adam right? Did my son kill all those people?'

'We each play the part we're given, Eve.'

I think of the boy who chose to starve rather than drink bone soup. Lucifer moves towards me. 'Time is running out, Eve. It is nearly dawn. I need your answer.'

'How long has he been your guest?'

'It is within your power to help him. Stand aside. Abandon your post and I will aid your son.'

'This is my last night, Lucifer. What does it matter? I promise I won't be back next year. Please, help Cain.'

Lucifer leaps across the bonfire to stand before me, invading my space. His eyes are glowing with intensity, and there is a feral twist to his lips. 'Giving up won't save your son but choosing me will.'

I look across the gap at Cain's bowed head, defeated shoulders. He sags against the demons holding him. To be given the power over his circumstance fills me with dread. I am not qualified to choose his fate. I would not willingly overturn the will of God, again. I fear that whatever I do, it will not be enough.

'How do I know if it is what he wants?'

'Do you not see him suffer?'

'You would have me suffer in his place. I could not live with the remorse if he resents me for interfering. My son has lived his life,' I choke the words out, 'made his choices, and never once sought me out. How can I know if he wants my help now?'

'Poor choices made in desperation, alone and unloved. Abandoned. Would you refuse him a second chance?'

I am no stranger to feeling alone and unloved. Lucifer chooses words to wound me the deepest.

21

DESPAIR

> Sisyphus, with immense labour, pushing the stone up the lofty hill, which ever, his labour lost, rolls back from the top, shows that men's miseries are endless.
>
> Phaedrus, *Appendix* 7.1–6

Lucifer extends his hand to me in a gallant gesture but this time there is no smile. 'I have declared my interest in you many times, Eve. I would prefer if you accept my offer without the need of this extra incentive, but I am not discouraged if Cain's predicament is the thing that tips the balance. I am the one who can make you happy. Trust me.'

'I want to talk to him.'

'He cannot pass through the gates. Mortal sinners don't enjoy the privilege of Samhain.'

'Then let me in.'

'You know that's not possible.'

That familiar ache of being so close to Cain but unable to reach him grinds away at my resolve.

'It's easy for you both to benefit. Speak the words,' Lucifer prompts.

I cannot win. To live in Lucifer's Eden, be his queen, and bear his demons, I must forsake God's pardon. If I remain steadfast in my faith, then I relinquish my dreams and the chance to save my son. I did nothing to save him last time. I am being given a second chance too.

I am too worn down to be angry at Lucifer's manipulations. I am ready to make my sacrifice.

'Set Cain free and I'll accept your offer.'

Lucifer sighs and shakes his head. 'That is beyond my power. I cannot pardon him for his transgressions, Eve. That is between Cain and God.'

'Then let me take his place. I shall suffer his torment and he will take mine on Earth. He can battle each Samhain in my stead. Take on my penance with God to earn forgiveness.'

'Penance is a sacrament, Eve. It is not in your power to transfer it to him. Each must make his own pact with God.' Lucifer pauses and steps back, regarding me with his amber eyes. 'After two thousand years, you are ready to walk away from one battle a year. Do you have the mettle to face the endless torments of Hell?'

He waves his hand and there is movement behind the gates. I see Cain struggling as demons surround him, herding him back to the depths.

'No, please. Not yet,' I cry out and drop to my knees. 'I have committed as many murders in God's name as Cain. I deserve to be in Hell with my son. If you cannot release him, take me too. I go willingly.'

There is fury in his gaze, and his voice trembles.

'You give your love to the wrong men, Eve. I offer to put you on a pedestal, a chance to end your suffering, and you refuse. Cain has brought you nothing but grief, yet you are so eager to throw your life and salvation away for him. What madness possesses you?'

'Tell me how I can save him?'

'You cannot. He is his mother's son. He suffers by choice.'

His words are as deadly as if he has drawn a blade. I look across the void and see my son is weeping and his tears are my undoing. My heart aches for Cain as it aches for myself.

Lucifer takes my hand, 'Say yes. I will ease his suffering. And yours. Don't hesitate.'

I push him away. He is too eager to help me. This act of showing more compassion than God, of taking care of me each battle. It lessens his responsibility for my plight. I know his words are designed to tug at my maternal instincts. After all these years of searching for my son I need to feel that the waiting has been worthwhile. I back away from Lucifer, watching for his reaction, my sword tight in my grasp. He is relaxed. Hopeful. My heels crunch on the coals that remain of the bonfire. I pivot and run across the burning embers towards the Gates of Hell for the first time in two thousand years.

I don't reach the gates—the generals block my way. They snarl and hiss, unsure what to do. I bare my teeth and raise my sword. One looks over my head, at Lucifer. I strike at that demon first. My sword bounces from his hide. It's madness, I know, but what do I have left?

I turn my sword on myself. If I kill myself, perhaps I will be condemned to the same hell as Cain.

There is a high-pitched whistle and demons come at me from all sides. I crumple under their weight. My sword arm is pinned to the ground. The weight increases as more pile on. I can't breathe enough to fill my lungs and the pressure on my ribs is immense. And that overwhelming grief comes in waves from their bodies into mine. As the darkness begins to take me over, I allow the tears to flow down my cheeks. I will never be with my son.

22

APATHY

> She doth tell me where to borrow
> Comfort in the midst of sorrow;
> Makes the desolatest place
> To her presence be a grace;
> And the blackest discontents
> Be her fairest ornaments.
> George Wither, *The Shepherd's Hunting*

THE COCK CROWS THREE TIMES TO HERALD THE morning. Lucifer, Bringer of Dawn, appears beside me. The sky behind him glows pale pink. He picks me up from the ground and carries me over the circle of scorched earth, back to my side of the battlefield. Smoke, the final offering from my bonfire, hangs like a black cloud over us. Small demons scurry past, rushing back to Hell before the gates slam shut. They spit on me and it burns like acid. These poison pock marks are nothing compared to the misery I already feel.

Lucifer places me gently on the ground and kneels beside me. My throat is parched, my eyes red and swollen, my chest hurts with every breath. He holds a cup of water to my lips. I drink, and when I am done, he dips his fingers in the water and gently bathes my eyes. He pours water on my wounds, washing away the grime. His fingers are cool salve against my burning skin. He chooses to do it this way, painstakingly and personal.

He works in earnest and I am nearly undone by his kindness. The worst of my injuries; the crushed ribs and spine, he kisses, healing them with his angel lips. He brings those lips to my temples and dulls my worst memories, blurs the faces of those I killed tonight.

Energy surges through my body with each gentle press of his flesh against my flesh. He fills me with light and life, restoring my physical health and my emotional state to stable. In those heartbeats, I absorb some of his divine invincibility. When he is finished, he sits back on his heels. As he moves beyond my reach, I feel the cool breeze of morning rush against my skin and yearn for his touch again. My humanity returns too swiftly with the throb of injury and the ache of defeat. I clutch at his arm, begging for more.

'You would not thank me for healing you completely, Eve.' There is a flash of sympathy in his eyes.

'Why did you do it? I want to destroy this body. I want to suffer like Cain.'

Over his shoulder I see dawn is here. The gates will close. Tears I cannot control trickle down my cheeks. He catches one on his fingertip.

'Then you will suffer the same fate as Adam, not Cain. There is no release there for you. And I've grown fond of this Eve.'

My tears blur my vision of his face, taut with concern. I am empty inside. I can have nothing I want and am doomed to this path designed for me by others.

'Time to say goodbye,' I say.

He grins but it doesn't reach his eyes. They are clouded and intense. His fingers tap gently against my breast. He knows where my heart lies.

His hand lingers over me. I reach out and take it, pulling it close. My skin burns for his touch. I don't want this to be the last time we are together.

'One last chance,' he whispers. 'Go on, Eve. Ask me.'

I should hate him. For what he did to me all those lifetimes ago. For what he did to Cain. For so many other things. What if?

'Pretend I already did,' I whisper.

He throws back his head and laughs. Loud and clear, it is the most wondrous sound in the world: angelic laughter. 'I can offer you choices but I can't make them for you.'

I nod. I know he's right. 'Everything is broken. The two things in my life that kept me going are both gone. I need...'

'I hate to see you like this. It makes me feel—'

'Guilty? It should.'

He shrugs and for the tiniest moment I catch a glimpse of uncertainty, before he shutters it away.

'—bored.'

'Very droll.'

'I thought you'd have figured it out by now.'

'What do you mean?'

He stands and walks away. Deprives me of his loveliness. That gnawing emptiness of withdrawal hits.

I lie there alone. Demon ichor is burning off with the light. I see the vapor rising, turning from black and grey to transparent tendrils that float away. No more smells of decay and mortification; the morning breeze freshens everything. It is a clean, new day.

I pull myself to sitting. My legs quake, my arms are

weak. But my wounds sport fresh pink skin—Lucifer's boon. It is time for me to leave. I hobble to my truck, heave the sword on the flatbed and yank open the door. I slump into the seat, shaking from that simple task, my muscles and nerves protesting. It takes a minute for my hands to still enough to put the key in the ignition. I turn the key but the engine just whirrs. I pump the clutch and try again. The engine catches, splutters and fails.

The Gates of Hell retreat to their camouflaged state behind the brick wall. The junkyard is back; cars, fridges and washing machines shimmering in the new day's wash. Brick and barbed wire basking in sunlight. Treacherous nature living in harmony with his illusion.

Lucifer stands by the brick wall. I try the engine again and it starts without issue. The radio comes to life too and Beyoncé tells me to put his things to the left. I grind the truck into gear and pull away.

I pass the sagging fence and the rickety gate and drive out into the desert. I resist the urge to glance in the rearview mirror. The sun is already fierce through the windshield and I wind down the window to catch what little breeze there is. It isn't long before the dusty track yields to tarmac and I turn onto the highway.

Cars pass me as I return to the real world. I drive and allow the tears to fall. Tears of frustration and revelation for all these wasted years. I curse the Nazarene and his blindness to the true nature of gods and angels, and my blindness in believing him.

I don't take my usual turnoff, instead I keep driving, on and up into the mountains. I don't know what I am looking for, only that I need to keep moving, to get far away. There has to be somewhere I can breathe more freely.

The road takes me higher where the air is sweet and

moist. I pull over at a lookout and get out to stretch my legs. The mountain air is cold and sharp. I lean against the low stone wall of the lookout and look down at the patchwork of fields. Beyond the fields lie tree-covered hills that stretch to the horizon. A giant shadow covers most of the land, cast by the mountain behind me.

I tap out a cigarette, but I don't light it. Smoking seems wrong here, at odds with the pine and loam of the land. I think about jumping. I think about Adam being reborn. I think about dying and how that sacrament is one I cannot experience.

Death comes when the sand runs out of the bag. Not knowing when the last grain of sand is reached is the true gift. Without this benediction, there is no satisfaction of lying on a deathbed with the solace of a good life lived.

I cannot experience death without going through the agony experienced by Adam, but that sensation of peace at the last moment is something I'd like to know. I think back to the time when I was close, in the wilderness. It was a turning point in my life. When I had lost Abel but didn't realize I had also lost Cain. Now I know he is gone. The wheel has turned again.

I lie on the ground and close my eyes.

It is cold, but I have endured worse. I lie with my legs and arms out straight, palms facing upward, fingers curled, knuckles touching the ground. I slow my breathing: *Savasana*, corpse pose. The final position.

I disengage myself physically, my limbs no longer feel my own. My breathing grows shallow and infrequent, only when necessary do I suck the smallest amount of air through my dry lips. The damp of the cold earth seeps through my clothes adding to that dank drain of death. I can feel myself slipping...

His hand is soft against my cheek. The lightest touch but it burns my skin, causing pain as he warms me, that pricking and poking of the return of circulation.

'Eve,' he whispers. 'You need to breathe.'

I sip at the air.

'More,' he insists.

I sip again but it hurts my lungs.

'What are you doing?' His voice is close to my ear, fragrant with apple and smoke.

'I want to experience death. To feel the change. Am I close?' My voice sounds weak and pathetic, sucked away by the air. I hear the sharp intake of his breath before he responds.

'If you were mortal, you would have passed by now.'

I open my eyes. The sky is too blue. The eagles ignore me as they circle high above, forming a halo around Lucifer's head.

'Saint Augustine said that the recollection of bodily death draws a man from sin and makes him humble.'

Lucifer smiles.

'Lack of humility is not a failing of yours, Eve.'

'Humility is needed when one faces the final judgment.'

'Ahh. I see you're working through the rulebook. You need not worry, Eve, there is no harsher judge on any firmament than your own conscience.'

That same conscience that let me waste two thousand years fighting for a cause that was always lost. The same conscience that let me believe I could defy God where Cain was concerned. My body is numb, I have no sensation other than heaviness. My mind is flying with the eagles, the sun is warm on their wings. I see through their eyes, two specks on the ground below, one lying, one kneeling. Translucent rays of light fan down around them. Divine light, *gloria celestis*. It is time to face my god.

'Lucifer?'

'Hmm?'

I open my eyes and stare into the starry depths of his. 'I am ready. Please take me to Uriel. To Him.'

His eyes cloud and he frowns, remaining completely still, more still than the mountain on which we perch. I am afraid he will deny me my request. I want to beg him but I force myself to stay silent and wait. My patience is stretched so thin but I am at the place where time teeters anyway. He nods. Once.

'Thank—' But he is gone.

No, that's not right.

I am gone.

23

HEARTSEASE

> For thus I read the meaning of this end:
> There are two ways of spreading light; to be
> The candle or the mirror that reflects it.
> I let my wick burn out—there yet remains
> To spread an answering surface to the flame
> That others kindle.
> Edith Wharton, 'Vesalius in Zante (1564)'

IT IS THOUSANDS OF YEARS SINCE I STOOD HERE AND although nothing looks the same, nothing feels changed. The valley beyond is no longer lush and a dusty wind blows from the west. I stand on the bank of a dry expanse that was once the mighty river Pishon. But I am facing Eden, where Uriel still stands sentinel with his flaming sword held high. Beyond him, past the cedar trees, now taller and wider, lies the entrance to the garden.

God trusts Uriel to keep his sanctuary safe. I trust him too, for it was he who buried Abel in Paradise. He is not a great conversationalist, unlike Lucifer. He spends too much time alone. A gatekeeper, like me, as Lucifer was quick to point out. If the task is good enough for Uriel, why did I resent it? Uriel, Prince of Presence, views me with bemused solemnity, waiting for me to speak. My throat is on fire as I struggle to form the words.

'I'm back.'

'So I see.'

'Can you tell Him I'm here?'

Uriel raises an eyebrow at my dirty, bloodied appearance and I wish I had thought to wash and change.

'He knows.'

Of course.

He comes like a rainstorm in the desert, a deluge that surpasses all expectation. The smell of life fills the air, and energy crackles over my skin, lifts my hair, as I am charged with power. I breathe deeply, hungry for restoration.

'Eve.' The word is an embrace. It hangs in the air between us. Expectant.

Disconcerted, I try not to fidget—not to appear the awkward teenager before a parent asking to borrow the car. There is so much at stake. I hesitate, afraid to speak out of turn, afraid I will anger Him. Afraid of rejection.

I pluck at my bloodied clothes. 'Have I done enough?'

'Do you wish to stop?' This circular questioning reminds me of Lucifer and I smile.

'Yes. I truly do.'

The silence is suffocating as I wait for His response. I wonder what He contemplates, why He needs to take any time at all when He is omniscient.

'Have I done enough?' I whisper the words again. The agony of waiting is worse than any battle wound. What if He says no or asks me to go back for another year? I don't know the protocol for negotiating with God.

'Do you believe you have?'

I blink back tears as I nod.

'So be it.'

Just like that. No argument. Without hesitation, He forgives me. I am surprised and disappointed at the speed of his absolution. His presence retreats and somehow the significance of my toil is reduced to unimportant.

I ate an apple. I lost a husband and two sons. I fought for two thousand years and carried the weight of sin for all of humankind on my back. There is no sense of victory, only a bitter taste.

'What happens now?' I stare at Uriel.

'You may enter.' He lowers his sword.

My prize, coveted for so long, is less shiny and without appeal, surrendered too easily without a fight. I feel cheated. Nothing is different now the burden of Original Sin is lifted. It was my motivation and now it has been stripped away. I expected a lightening of the load, but all I feel is lack.

For so long, my life has been about achieving forgiveness and finding Cain. Without those goals what am I? The Earth holds no further allure with Cain in Hell. I wonder how my absolution will affect humans, if they will share my emptiness or welcome their freedom as a blessing. If it will strengthen their resolve against demons on future Samhains.

Uriel waves his hand, gesturing towards the gates.

There are no further obstacles. Absolved of sin and within steps of my dream, I don't know why I hesitate to enter. It should be easy to go back, but it is not. No longer am I the Eve who walked in this Garden, unaware of any other existence. Nor am I the Eve who sought penance for the Sin into which she was manipulated. I am not even the Eve I was last night as I resolved to end my procrastination. I am Eve who is schooled in new ways.

I was programmed to be subservient but have corrupted my original programming. Returning to Eden will restore me. Take away the corruption.

Uriel clears his throat, waiting. I am struck by the resemblance he bears to Lucifer. The way the light seems to seek them both out. The way my heart beats faster in his presence. But Uriel exudes a sense of stability, not danger.

'Eden awaits,' he says.

I don't move and Uriel tilts his head. Again, I am reminded of Lucifer.

'May I take a moment to say goodbye?'

I walk down to the dry riverbed, far enough to give the illusion of privacy from His all-seeing presence. Under my breath, I whisper Lucifer's name and he comes at once. Nonchalant and relaxed, his hands in his pockets, one shoulder raised slightly in question. He wears a lopsided smile as he extends his hand to take mine. An inadequate farewell after all we've shared.

'Halloween won't be the same,' he says.

It hits me that I will never see him again. Lucifer is no longer allowed in my future home. My torment must have shown on my face, for he steps closer, pulls me against him and kisses me hard on the mouth. I cling to him, breathing him in. He has been the worst of adversaries and the best of friends and I will miss him. Hot tears prick my eyes.

'Don't cry.' He produces a white handkerchief. 'It's what you want.'

I am no longer certain it is. So much has changed since I struck this bargain. The years fighting against Lucifer's horde have shaped me. He pushed me beyond my limitations, chipped away at long-held beliefs and plundered new depths.

I hold his face in my hands, trying to commit every detail to memory. My prevailing recollection of the Garden is not one of God, nor of Adam. It is of Lucifer feeding me fruit.

'It won't be the same in there without you,' I say.

'Safer.' He grins.

'Is safer what I want?'

I know once I step into the Garden, my doubts and anxieties will disappear. Peace will soothe all my ills, take away the emptiness and hurt I carry deep inside. My days and nights will be blissful and without want. I am a slow learner.

Returning to Eden means giving up much I have come to value. That simplicity I craved for so long now sounds like a subjugation to ignorance. I thought I wanted security, but the price is the loss of my independence. After surviving alone, it feels wrong to abrogate all responsibility and accountability for my wellbeing and happiness to another. Experience has refashioned me. I no longer long for oblivion.

I take Lucifer's hand and walk towards Eden.

Uriel raises his sword.

'Your paradise awaits, but you must enter alone,' Uriel says.

'I've changed my mind,' I say.

'Why?'

'I don't want to become less than I am.'

'God's presence diminishes you?' Uriel doesn't understand.

'Yes. I was reborn the day I left Eden. The years of wandering were my childhood. The years of fighting my adolescence. I finally know who I am. To return to Eden is to abandon my growth. I will become His version of me, not mine.'

There is a rumble of thunder overhead. Uriel looks up, his expression is one of concentration, of listening to something. He looks back at me, his mouth grim and his voice stern.

'Lucifer twists your perspective,' he says. 'He seduces you with his charm. Think carefully before you walk away.'

'And if God didn't want that to happen why did He entrust me into his care all these years?'

There is another rumble of thunder. Far away. Lucifer gives a whoop of laughter. His crow of victory. He raises my hand to his lips and his eyes meet mine. There is that look; the one of the inveterate gambler whose horse wins the race at long odds. He can no more deny his nature than I can mine. To Lucifer I am no more than a wager. A pawn tossed about in his rivalry with God. Having learned their rules, I see that I no longer need to follow them, for if I participate in their game, I will always be less than them. There is nothing for me to gain from either side. They can't give me what I am looking for.

All my years of searching for answers and I have them. Lucifer's temptations, God's silence, Adam's indifference, Lilith's intrusions, and Cain's rejection—they were the tools I needed to forge the woman I am. By accepting how things are, I can see how it is meant to be. How I manifest my world, be it with sorrow or joy, makes no difference to anyone but me. All life is sorrowful, Buddha says, for sorrow is the precursor to joy, and I am joyful at my revelation.

Lucifer puts his arm around my shoulders.

'Let's go,' he says.

I take a last long look at the familiar lines of his face and trace my thumb over his full lips.

'Eve?' He is wary.

'Thank you for everything,' I say.

He grips my upper arms, his fingers digging into my flesh.

'You need me. I'm the only one who can give you what you want.' He flashes that million-dollar grin. 'Eden with me in it.'

I gently extract myself from his grasp. My fears are gone, replaced by exhilaration. I have the courage to turn from God's path and the strength to avoid Lucifer's.

'Goodbye, Lucifer. Take care of yourself,' I say.

He growls at me.

I turn to Uriel and smile. He smiles back. It is the first time I've seen him smile and it brings a youthfulness to his features.

'Farewell, Eve,' he says.

I look out beyond the riverbed, over the valley to the haze of green on the horizon. I start walking towards unclaimed territory. The perfect place to create a garden of my own.

ACKNOWLEDGMENTS

My deepest thanks to the talented and generous individuals who have helped me bring this book together. I name but a few; James Bradley, L.E.Daniels, Anita Mumm, Kelly Rigby, Anna Caswell, Andi Spark, Marianna Shek, Helen Petrovic and Joelene Pynnonen.

Thank you to my writing groups—Triune Writers, The Very Hardworking Writers, Vision Writers, and the Friday club at the Queensland Writers' Centre—for suffering through early drafts, rewrites, and offering unwavering support. I am blessed to have you in my corner.

Sharita Russell.
May 2021

ABOUT THE AUTHOR

Sharita Russell is a writer of fantasy and magical realism. Original Sinner is Sharita Russell's debut novel. If you would like to receive information about forthcoming novels and interviews :

Click here

https://www.sharitarussell.com

 facebook.com/sharitarussellauthor
 instagram.com/sharitarussell
 twitter.com/sharita_russell

Lightning Source UK Ltd.
Milton Keynes UK
UKHW011542200821
389183UK00003B/990